JUN   2002

Women About Town

Women
About Town

LAURA JACOBS

VIKING

VIKING
Published by the Penguin Group
Penguin Putnam Inc., 375 Hudson Street, New York, New York 10014, U.S.A.
Penguin Books Ltd, 80 Strand, London WC2R 0RL, England
Penguin Books Australia Ltd, 250 Camberwell Road, Camberwell,
   Victoria 3124, Australia
Penguin Books Canada Ltd, 10 Alcorn Avenue,
   Toronto, Ontario, Canada M4V 3B2
Penguin Books (N.Z.) Ltd, Cnr Rosedale and Airborne Roads, Albany,
   Auckland, New Zealand

Penguin Books Ltd, Registered Offices:
Harmondsworth, Middlesex, England

First published in 2002 by Viking Penguin,
a member of Penguin Putnam Inc.

10 9 8 7 6 5 4 3 2 1

PUBLISHER'S NOTE
This is a work of fiction. Names, characters, places, and incidents are either the prod-
uct of the author's imagination or used fictitiously, and any resemblance to actual per-
sons, living or dead, business establishments, events, or locales is entirely coincidental.

LIBRARY OF CONGRESS CATALOGING IN PUBLICATION DATA
Jacobs, Laura.
   Women about town / Laura Jacobs.
       p.   cm.
   ISBN 0-670-03088-0
       1. New York (N.Y.)—Social life and customs—Fiction.   2. Women—
New York (State)—New York—Fiction.   I. Title.
   PS3610.A356 W66 2002
   813'.54—dc21   2001056788

This book is printed on acid-free paper. ∞

Printed in the United States of America
Set in Fairfield with Didot
Designed by Carla Bolte

To my father

EDWARD JESSE JACOBS

and my mother

ANN

Acknowledgments

The author wishes to express her gratitude to Alice Martell, her agent, who championed this book and these characters with such passion; her editor, Pamela Dorman, for inspired, and inspiring, guidance; her editors at *Vanity Fair*, Graydon Carter and Aimée Bell, for making the magazine such a nurturing home; and, most of all, her husband, James Wolcott, who read the first few pages of what would be this book and said, "Keep going."

Contents

Women About Town

Dust

Iris Biddle was wrestling with six little sconce shades, a set commissioned by a high-handed broker on Bleecker Street. She was trying to re-create a glow she once found in a flea market shade. The silk was beige—a dark, men's-club beige—but over a lightbulb it had shone amber with a lovely pinkish cast, even though there wasn't a pink thread anywhere in the weave. Iris knew such complex color came with age, a good forty years in a room with cigarette smoke, liquor, humidity, dust, lust, certainly love (kisses near the curtains; a bit more, maybe, on the leather chesterfield after midnight). It was impossible to re-create age—as impossible as re-creating youth, no matter what the creams and salves and lotions promised to women around the world. Age, anyway, was more interesting.

Iris had dust to spare in her third-floor Gramercy Park

apartment. Every woman had to come to terms with dust. Men never seemed to see it—dust on the windowsill, dust floating into your nose, dust secreted in pockets and pants cuffs (how did it get there?). Iris had to be careful about dust in a room full of expensive silk. She had to remember to cover her work at night. Even if she blew lightly on a lamp shade—to blow the new dust off—she had to control her breath so that there was no moisture in it. Even one fine water spot could stain.

Sometimes Iris wondered if working with such fragile materials was really the right career for her. Didn't it encourage a tendency toward the finicky? Oh, of course she loved "rust and crust," the term her designer friends used for objects peeling, spotted, practically rotting with age, things like old tassels going bald before your eyes, or old picture frames with the gold leaf chipped. In the flea market Iris snapped up scraps of antique silk, faded and frayed by decades of morning sun through windows. She thought these muted silks were romantic, like ruins in a painting. Sometimes, at the edge or in a corner, a streak of the original dye survived, which was fascinating, a bonus. It showed exactly what time and sun had done. But Iris couldn't forgive herself if she added to the ruin. If she further chipped the frame or frayed the fabric she berated herself for not being careful enough, for being a bad guardian. She hated to make mistakes, because then the thing wasn't what it had been, and had to be fixed, if it could be. And even when no one could see the fix, Iris secretly knew, and it nagged at her. This strange tension, not quite rational as Iris was the first to admit, had hovered over her ever since childhood, like a strange second moon. But then, as people were always telling her, Iris was a classic Virgo.

She remembered, for instance, the pencils, two for each student, handed out on the first day of first grade. It was so grown-up, two long perfect pencils, so exciting—until she saw the pencils had no erasers! No, the teacher had told them, you don't get erasers until the second grade; you must learn to be careful in your writing. They were instructed to cross out their mistakes, but instead Iris tried to erase them by wetting her finger and rubbing the page, which left an angry gray smudge and sometimes almost a rip within the smudge. She remembered that teacher, a stale string bean, standing over her during penmanship one day, then snatching up her workbook and holding it open to the class, saying, "Iris thinks she's better than the rest of us and doesn't make mistakes. But look at this." Well, everyone knew she was Mean Old Mrs. Brown. Still, Iris was mortified.

And then there were those first months of her period. She didn't get it until she was fifteen, and wasn't really eager for it, seeing her girlfriends rocking in pain in the gym-class locker room, cradling their cramps, moaning about "the curse." When it did finally come she felt she had been slain. Those napkins they wore then, an inch thick, you safety-pinned this thing to your underpants, or worse, attached it to an elastic belt, a kind of garter belt for napkins that hugged it up against you where it grew warm and dense. It had made her think of the family's standard poodle, Sadie, who wore a similar contraption when she went into heat. It wasn't until freshman year of college, when Iris finally braved a tampon, that she stopped feeling like Sadie.

I changed those pads every half hour, Iris recalled, the

minute a drop of blood fell. At fifteen Iris had thought if she
could keep the napkin spotless the flow would stop. But of
course, she learned as everyone does that the blood, the dust,
the smoke, the flow never stop.

Iris needed a perfect white blouse. She had been needing a perfect white blouse forever it seemed. Iris had three
white blouses hanging in her closet, but they just weren't right
somehow. The Romeo Gigli with a wide-set collar was still stylish, but not much fun to wear. It tended to loop down over
one shoulder like a slipped harness or a too large halo. The
sweet white painter's smock was now maybe too sweet, or too
Bohemian—too something. The oversized man-tailored shirt
was crisp and ready, but Waspy-sporty was a rare mood for Iris,
too starched and standard-issue. Iris would see these three
whites hanging together and turn away from them with that
feeling of disappointment one so often feels when turning
away from one's clothes. Failed again by the find that was exact
and exciting a year ago and now looks inherited from someone
stupid.

"Why won't you go away?" Iris had asked the man-tailored
when she last surveyed it for stains, though she knew there
would be a day when she would want to, would need to, wear
it, and she'd be thankful for its patience. She'd hung it back
up, pulled out the smock and tossed it into the thrift shop bag.
She was always culling her clothes. Getting them out often felt
better than bringing them in. I'm not this, I'm not that. What
am I?

In her thirties, after she moved back to Manhattan, Iris
could spend hours browsing in thrift shops. For some rea-

son the smell of dust and mildew, the scent of woolens limp in the unmistakable grip of mothballs—that death sachet—these didn't bother her, so caught up was she in the hunt, the secret rescue of beautiful workmanship She Alone Understood. She kept a sharp eye out for an unlabeled Charles James, shoes by Roger Vivier, anything by Geoffrey Beene. But she also had a deep respect for the union ladies, and a special fondness for the well-bred buttonholes they used to do—covered buttonholes.

"No one," Iris had announced more than once, as if it were the last straw on Judgment Day, "covers buttonholes anymore." It was a sublime form of finish, a tricky technique that covered its own tracks. You could look and look at this kind of buttonhole, and it looked right back at you, an upper and lower lid of fabric through which the button would slide cleanly, in a wink. You couldn't see how it was constructed unless you ripped the lids from their seams, a destruction Iris had allowed herself just once and then regretted. These days every covered buttonhole was precious. They were so time-consuming even the Parisians didn't make them anymore.

And then Iris had had it with thrift shops. She'd been passing by Council Thrift, run by wrinkled widows with vinegar voices, and she swerved in by habit. She was in a bad mood, sullen about her sluggish finances, appalled by the superrich clients who couldn't help treating her like a tradeswoman even though they came to her because she was an artist. She was soon to turn forty and the shop's bad breath and dime-store tags suddenly taunted her. I'm browsing with bag ladies, she realized. Iris never again set foot in a thrift shop, except to drop things off.

And anyway, she had begun seeing beyond the clothes in those bins and racks, reading the tea leaves, so to speak, the lives of perfectionists before her. She once saw six brocade dresses all in a row, all made by the same Hong Kong tailor in the same Empire style with the same stand-up collar and the same three-inch hem. None looked like it had ever been worn, or worn much. Iris hadn't been able to shake the image of these six princess dresses, custom-made and untouched. Had the owner suffered a sudden death? Or a fear of life, with its spills and spots, the bump and splash of champagne, the inevitable half-moons steeping under the armholes? And wasn't a fear of mess its own kind of death? Had the owner habitually reached for those dresses in her closet, fingered them, and decided no, they were more important to her unblemished, as symbols of plenty? Sometimes, in the sad racks where the shoes were kept, heels run down and toes curling up, Iris would see the collection of some matron with a weakness for Saks or Delman, immaculate pairs of pumps with two-inch heels, Fenton lasts, a satin bow here, a rhinestone buckle there—variations on the theme of Stately Restraint. For those who thought exquisite taste and disciplined upkeep could ensure against the grave, a trip to the thrift shop was edifying.

"Do not store up treasure upon earth, where moth and rust do corrupt, and thieves break in and steal." This line had mesmerized Iris in Sunday school. Matthew 6:19. She had underlined it in her Bible, and read it at home in her room, frequently, possessively, feeling the whole of her being focused in on those words. But why had she so loved this verse? Iris couldn't quite say. The treasure and the moths? The Aesop's fable sitting inside the Apostles? As a child Iris had read all of Aesop and knew all the morals. Her favorite fable was The Dog in the Manger, and to this day when she came upon something wonderful at Bergdorf's or Saks, something so on sale it made her greedy even though it wasn't really her style, she would think, "do not begrudge others of that which you cannot use yourself . . ." and would leave it, she hoped, for its rightful buyer.

But Matthew. Was it the word "corrupt"—so alarming it was attractive? Had she known already, at the age of twelve, the truth of that insinuating word, that mortal forces were everywhere unseen, weaving, rending? Iris had grown up in a haze of innocence, but she had never been innocent of her luck. It was a sheltered childhood, a secure world created by a father and mother who took pleasure in the job, both of them first-generation successes, enjoying doing it right. Dr. and Mrs. Saroyan, her father dashing, dark, her mother a whipped-cream blonde of Hungarian descent, hair soft as spun sugar. Their vivacious adulthood encircled the children's realm like elegant trees too tall to climb. Iris watched as other childhoods—her best friend Leslie's, or that silent girl at the stable, Kathy's—tore softly open, as spiderwebs do when they catch an insect too big and kicking. Iris felt strongly what her friends didn't have compared to her. And when she went through her shy, gawky, teenage years, friends blossoming around her, cheeky and rosy, she thought, but they deserve it, to make up for the cold father, the mother who drinks, the parents there but not there.

When her own father died when she was twenty-three, a

cancer that took him blithely in ten months, leaving the family stunned, locked in loss, Iris still would not allow herself to view it as a tragedy. Tragedy was mud slides in Bangladesh. It was the school bus going off the bridge. It was not someone's father of fifty-three, joyful in his prime, revered by his colleagues, adored all around, trimming his Dunhill cigar with clean surgeon's fingers as he argued aesthetics with his eldest daughter, infuriating her, egging her on to do better, his Swarthmore girl in a black turtleneck who'd finally grown into her lashy eyes and fine nose and skin pale as bleached parchment against dark hair, and who wanted to please and impress him though maybe not in that order. A doctor's death at fifty-three, that was tough luck, a cruel blow, not tragedy really, but life. Besides, they'd been so blessed to have had him in the first place.

Just last week that line from Matthew had come back to Iris. Feeling cornered by those six little sconce shades and the pushy woman who wanted them too soon, Iris had succumbed to all sorts of impulses. She hemmed a pair of boring black pants way up above the ankles; ordered a fifty-dollar matinee ticket (much too much) for the new Tom Stoppard play; reorganized her scarf drawer, then pulled out a favorite cashmere, wrapped it around her neck, and went for a sit in Gramercy Park, where it was her and the green-card nannies with their platinum-card charges. It was the last day of August, gray and unseasonably cool. A high wind was pushing around the ancient trees in the tiny private park ("a postage stamp" was the way Iris described it to out-of-town friends, though she really thought of it as an emerald in a Victorian ring box).

The little weeping willow that stood by the caretaker's shed was whipping gracefully back and forth. It's like a silvery school of fish, Iris thought, that can't decide which way to go. She watched the nannies chat, their hair blowing, their blouses billowing. They were surprisingly blasé, she thought, about what was possibly a storm coming. Iris swept her own hair back from her face and stared upward, losing herself in the drama of wind and leaves, the trees flush, rustling, like great ladies in green taffeta. Then she stopped on one tree, one that must be dying. The branches were bare, stark, hardly moving in the wind. How was it Iris had never noticed this tree before? Such a delicate web of boughs and knots and air, it made her feel *for* the bare branches, made her feel she too was a bare branch, all alone in the air, and made her want to possess, to own, the beauty of those branches. But how?

When Iris returned to her apartment she folded the scarf carefully, admiring the ivory pinstripes on the soft celadon background and discovering, dismayed, moth holes near the fringe. Even with cedar chips in the drawer, the scarf hadn't been safe. She went to the bookcase for the Bible she knew was there somewhere. She wanted to see those old lines from Matthew—she couldn't remember how the passage ended. She found the book far back on the highest shelf and had to blow a gray layer of dust off the top. The gilt-edged pages were thin and slippery, making a fluttery sound, like that typing paper everyone used in college, onionskin.

"But lay up for yourselves treasures in heaven, where neither moth nor rust doth corrupt, and where thieves do not break through nor steal. For where your treasure is, there will your heart be also."

Iris knew "treasure" must mean love of God, and that one's love of others flowed from that. Of course she wouldn't presume to disagree with Matthew. And yet, Iris wasn't sure she could completely agree either. Objects could have a kind of soul; they could have meaning. There were intense reverberations between people and things. She'd never forgotten the look of tenderness a young milliner had given her "Cecil Beaton" shade (admittedly, a rather obvious confection in Belle Epoque black and white with black-and-white silk pompoms), the way his gentle fingers reached for those pompoms, and the happiness with which he'd written the last of three five-hundred-dollar checks, a layaway arrangement.

Iris knew she was supposed to be married and raising kids. She knew her friends feared for her, turning forty and the clock ticking and she seeming so introverted. Yes she could still have children. But Iris couldn't let herself think about that now, the little wet mouth latched to her breast, the little fist around her finger . . .

She was single. She could barely make ends meet just taking care of herself. If she were to have a child, it had to have a father as good as her own. She couldn't compromise on that. No. And she couldn't dwell on it either. Or nothing would get done. Iris—she would say to herself on Madison Avenue, when the window of Bonpoint caught her eye, all those sweet little Peter Pan collars—there's no point in stopping so keep walking. Iris—when she saw families on Fridays packing their cars with groceries for the weekend house—you have things to do too. Iris, she told herself now, you need a white blouse.

This time she would design it herself. She would go to West Fortieth Street for fabric, something light yet stiff, like whipped egg whites. Silk organdy, maybe, or paper taffeta. She would find the fabric and take it to the tailor. Nothing made life simpler than a perfect white blouse.

Northeast Corridor

Lana Burton was on the train back from Boston. She had taken a long weekend to visit her best friend, Megan, and was now comfy in a window seat, heading south, looking east. She had brought work to do on the five-hour ride up and back: a new book on the role of hick towns in the American musical, which she was reviewing for one of those in-flight magazines. But Lana knew even as she packed it that the book didn't stand a chance. Instead, on the ride up, she went page by page through *Vogue* and *Harper's Bazaar*, magazines she rarely bought except when traveling by plane or train—they made the trip more glamorous, more Elizabeth Taylor and Richard Burton in *The V.I.P.s* (did people, Lana wondered, know what those letters stood for anymore?). And on the ride back down, on a Sunday afternoon, in an odd sort of suspended animation, she would just drift, taking in the world outside the train's wide window, a succession of bays and inlets and docks that would eventually end with the long tunnel into Penn Station.

Lana was studying the houses, the wealthy ones, white with shutters, gabled and well maintained. They were situated up and away on hills, so as to be above the water and in a position to see over the horizon. It was a good metaphor, Lana thought, the long view that money afforded, the sight lines—like sitting in the grand tier at the Metropolitan Opera. Closer to the tracks, the houses were ramshackle affairs, big boxes that would have been at home on the Great Plains, or little bungalows with lots of rusty old stuff in the backyard, like a lawn sale that was never going to take place. Lana smiled, thinking what her boyfriend Sam had said when she described these yards after her last trip north: "I see the same backyards on the way to Baltimore. It's like the houses ate too much junk and burped it all up." Sam could be on the quiet side in a group, but with Lana he was a fount of observation.

I couldn't even afford one of these crummy bungalows, Lana thought. She had never cared about houses, not the way so many people care, how it defined who you are and where you stand, et cetera. She'd always assumed she would have a house, something like her family's stone house under shady elms in Evanston, Illinois (the "Honorable" house, her friends called it, because her dad was a federal judge). But heading back to her studio apartment on West Fifty-fifth Street, five hundred square feet that would be dark and stuffy and double locked when she returned, Lana had to admit that a house, any house, was not in the big picture these days. And she did feel a wistfulness when she was at Megan's, a path not taken, though she preferred to think of it as a path postponed.

In the old Victorian that Megan and her husband were renovating slowly and meticulously, cream with green shutters and a half acre of forest right next to it, Megan would serve cocktails in the living room, and sometimes, like last night, an early October evening, dinner on the screened porch. *A screened porch!* And all those screen doors! Until you'd lived in New York City you really couldn't appreciate the freedom of a screen door, the squinch and bang it made, a sound that was native language in the spacious suburbs where it ran counterpoint to the crickets. And then there was Megan's studio, in a sort of square cupola on the roof, where light showered in—"actually too much light," Megan said—which meant she could only work up there at certain hours when the sun was between windows, which suited her fine because, as Megan explained, "children don't want you to do your own work. You have to jigsaw yourself in. Momentum? Concentration? Forget it."

"But everything seems to flow anyway," Lana had said, envious of that sun-drunk room, its whitewashed floorboards mottled with pastel sprays and arcs, the spring showers Megan made shaking out her brushes (before the baby, it was pungent oils that took ages to dry, after the baby, easy-to-clean watercolors). When Lana wrote her freelance theater reviews she had to do it after hours, in her tiny office at the showbill magazine where she was senior editor. She would stay late, her computer screen aglow, intensified by the night outside (for dinner, egg-drop soup from around the corner, with an order of rice dumped in). Or she would come back on weekends, when the place looked like an abandoned ship, quiet for miles. She'd gotten used to writing at the office.

"No flow," Megan said shaking her head. "It's an illusion." But it wasn't. The work Megan was currently doing up in her cupola—watercolors painted with eyeliner-fine brushes, swift and intricate—were like game boards of domestic imagery. A fried egg, a tin globe, a diaphragm, a dog bowl, a clock, etc. Megan would arrange these kinds of things in a spiral or a checkerboard or like the Monopoly square, and even as you tried to figure out the connections you felt something fleeting, a guessing game played with Time. Megan was getting the stop-start rhythm of her life into her pictures.

"Let's put it this way," said Lana. "You have a million windows and I'm lucky to have three. Two big and one little. And the little one is frosted so it doesn't even count."

"Well you don't need windows! You have New York at your fingertips. Do you have any idea how much time I spend *in the kitchen?*" They were in the kitchen when Megan said it and it was true, Lana didn't envy all those square meals Megan had to make.

They were both thirty-four, had met sophomore year of college, Megan a laid-back beauty (socially a ten), Lana the girl Friday type (she put herself at seven, sometimes eight). They weren't in the same circles, but one afternoon they were both in the dorm lounge and could hear that Julio Iglesias song down the hall, "To All The Girls I've Loved Before." A fellow student walked into the lounge, took a yogurt out of the mini-fridge, stood, listened, and sighed to the ceiling, "I love his humanity," then walked out of the lounge. Lana and Megan looked at each other, their friendship catching in the moment both realized they were amused and appalled for the same reason.

"It's that 'before' that makes it especially obnoxious," said Megan.

"It just hangs there," said Lana. "Before what? Before the next girl and the next and the next. It's about *groupies*."

"I know," said Megan. "And this is the song women are swooning over. *Humanity?*"

"I know," said Lana. "More like Hugh Hefner!"

Soon their homework was suffering as they skipped classes to meet at the student center where they ate too many greasy grilled cheeses, drank endless cups of coffee, discussed men, art, and life like French philosophers, and occasionally wondered if they weren't being pretentious (they usually decided they weren't, just "avid to understand"—they loved the word "avid"; it sounded exactly like what it was). The friendship was born full-blown, complete with rules never spoken: when they were twinged by what the other had that they didn't, they said so, in a joke or complaint or straight on. Saying it made it okay, irrelevant.

"For the record," Lana said, watching Megan whip up side dishes out of Jacques Pépin, "when did you even learn to make a square meal?" In their twenties, when they were sharing an apartment in Chicago—the messy two-bedroom that Megan's med-school boyfriend (now doctor husband) called the "crash pad for girls"—Megan had one recipe that doubled as a specialty. It was a chicken curry thick as stroganoff, a pale orange that suggested—falsely, it always turned out—a Creamsicle version of curry. It was very good, but spicy, not the melting ambrosia you expected it would be. "The taste never matched the color," Lana said. Megan, who never let her ego get in the way of the truth, would nod. "I don't make it much anymore. It's too wonky." Which always got Lana laughing—the way Megan said "wonky."

Anyway, Lana could tease because she had no specialty to her name, she'd been too busy running out for eight o'clock curtains, doing what you do if you want to be a critic—seeing everything, theater on Lincoln Avenue, dance at the Auditorium, opera at the Lyric, concerts at Orchestra Hall. In those days, when she told people she wanted to be a fine arts critic, they just looked at her baffled. How do you become that? they would ask. Is there a school you go to? No, she would answer, you just see everything and write reviews (she was writing them for the city's free weekly, the *Chicago Reader*, for a measly thirty-five dollars apiece, but the exposure was worth it). During the day Lana was an assistant editor for the show-bill magazine that was in all the theaters, a real mom-and-pop operation, but it did give her access to lots of free tickets (and amazingly, they did have a New York office!). My Formative Years in Chicago, Lana mused. The train was slowing, pulling into Mystic, Connecticut, which always made Lana think of the movie *Mystic Pizza*, one of those coming-of-age movies about who stays in town and who doesn't.

It wasn't supposed to be Lana living in New York. It was going to be Lana's older sister Livia. But isn't that the way things often worked out? The ambition of the one you admire somehow becomes your ambition too? And it wasn't even on purpose. Lana wouldn't begin to compete with her older sister. Livia was one of those enchanted creatures: picture pretty, a silky Breck Girl brunette, surrounded by friends, but sensitive in private, not always up to her aura, soft inside. Maybe it had to do with being a twin. It was always Tom and Olivia, never Livia and Tom. You couldn't ask for a nicer older brother and sister—six years older, a big gap. (Home one day with flu, so bored in bed she decided to sit hidden on the stairs listening to her mother's bridge game, Lana heard her own name mentioned and then her mother's voice, a jolt of comic timing, "What can I say? William had just brought down the gavel on a *loooong* case . . ." This followed by titters from the ladies. It was definitely not the story—"we wanted to give the baby crib one last go"—Lana had always been told.) Despite the gap, her brother and sister tried to include her. Lana looked up to them, and from her angle she could see that Tom was as easygoing as Livia was self-questioning.

So she was careful with Livia. For the one year they shared a room—and Lana could see perfectly well that it wasn't easy for a thirteen-year-old to share with a seven-year-old—Lana walked on eggs. She remembered listening to musicals at night in the dark with her older sister, each in her twin bed, ears alert, four feet of space between them but both listening to the click, whir, drop, pause, and static crackle of the needle on the outer rim of the record and then the joyous first chords of the next overture as *Oklahoma!* cropped up "high as an elephant's eye" or *My Fair Lady* swooped into bloom. And Lana's delight as Livia sang along—"All I want is a room somewhere"—with a raw Cockney accent, and Lana keeping extra still because it was so lovely listening to Livia sing. Lana was happy to be the audience, even though she might have liked to sing too, because it was delicious to be included in Livia's life.

Both Tom and Livia had wonderful voices, inherited from their father who let himself sing beautifully in church, a rather florid baritone that used to embarrass Lana, it seemed to her the vocal equivalent of his Sunday aftershave. (Like their mother, Lana had good pitch but a thin voice, so she took ballet, a mute art she could make her own, even if she wasn't ever invited into the first row in class, the row where the ballerinas-to-be mesmerized the mirror.) When the twins were in high school, taking part in spring shows, pushing back the living room furniture for at-home rehearsal, Lana was promoted from audience to coach and was grilled on details of their performances. Tom was always the same, sailing through on charisma and a rolling tenor voice. ("There's one in every high school," he liked to say now.) Livia was always stopping to start again, to get not just the notes but the tone, the emotion, to be not herself but the character. She could get exasperating, but Lana saw even then that Livia's presence was more interesting, more reaching and flickering, than Tom's. They were like Mickey Rooney and Judy Garland, Lana secretly thought, in those old show-in-a-barn movies—a bee and a moth.

Once her parents were in the living room when Lana, ten at the time, rendered a verdict. "Tom," she said, "maybe if you weren't so good at this song, it would be better." Her father looked at her carefully and said, "Lana's a little Solomon," and her mother nodded. "She's very tactful." Lana, dumb with pride, took the compliment as her cross. Livia, on the other hand, eventually did as countless women had done before her, she traded her dream of Broadway for marriage, a coach house in Kenilworth, and the dreams of her children to come. And never once seemed to regret it. This from the girl who wept for a week when she didn't get Maria in *West Side Story*, senior year (she got Anita, because Tom was the only possible Tony and the drama teacher couldn't cast a brother and sister as star-crossed lovers).

It turned out it was Lana who had to have the stage. Not in the way they did, not being on it. Lana loved its curtained world of overtures and entrances, soliloquies and dream sequences, climaxes and codas and the silence at the end (drowned out these days by people who clapped too soon, not knowing that silence was the last note of every show). Each production was a mystery to be solved. It wasn't just a matter of saying whether the show worked or not. The real question was *how* did it work, or *why* did it fail, and *what burned true?* Crouched over a computer keyboard, under lamplight, Lana would answer with her own performance—on the page. She'd respond with her own soliloquies, her own codas, her own full voice in final judgment. It was frightening. And fun. Lana knew she had a flair for it. Plus, the will. People, she learned, resented you picking apart performances they liked. When she found herself face-to-face with someone who was going on about a movie or play she'd basically hated, Lana would usually just ask questions. What did you like most about it? Have you seen that director's work before? She felt herself go beige, like a lizard on a log, because she didn't want to hurt the person's feelings or make them mad at her. Deep down, Lana knew she would end up in New York. A city where they argued about the arts. And respected critics.

But she wasn't one yet. In Chicago she had made a little name for herself as an up-and-comer, in New York she was just another freelancer, looking for a gig. The train was slowing into New Haven, which always made Lana think of Cole Porter at Yale—Whiffenpoofs and letter sweaters. In New Haven the train would shut off for twenty minutes while they changed the engine. Should Lana eat the sandwich Megan had packed for her, or wait until they were moving again? For some reason, it seemed better to eat while the train was moving. I should be able to explain why that is, Lana told herself, but she wasn't sure she could. Maybe it's more of a picnic, more festive, as we hurtle along. Maybe when we're sitting in the station, it feels furtive to be chewing, like breaking some rule of style. It's sad-sack. Still, Lana was starving, hadn't eaten since breakfast around eight o'clock—toast and coffee—with another coffee from the club car, and now it was twoish. The second the train slid out of the station, Lana unwrapped the sandwich, chicken and mustard on sourdough bread. That was the thing about a best friend. They remembered details—the mustard—that even your own mother forgot. "Do you want mayonnaise?" Lana's mom would ask, to which Lana would say, incredulous, "I can't believe you're asking me that. I have never once since the day I was born taken mayonnaise on *anything*." Mom was smart, but she could be spacey too. Lana would call home tonight, to check in.

It was autumn out the window, the sky a cool blue, the leaves on trees going yellow, some already curled and brown, the brown of paper bags. It was homecoming weather. Lana remembered when she first heard Tom and Livia talk about homecoming. They were high school freshmen. She had never heard the word before but they spoke it excitedly and knowingly, as if it were something obvious and important. Suddenly the house was abuzz with the homecoming parade, and the game and the dance, so Lana started feeling the excitement of homecoming too, even though she had no idea what it was. Who was coming home? She went to the parade with her parents, stood on the curb with the crowd, and watched for Tom and Livia and the freshman float. Leaves blew in swirls, scratching in the street. The cheerleaders bounced by in their short blue skirts, knees pink and dimpled with the chill, white wool flashing in the pleats. Lana could still hear the nasal bray of the high school band (well, all high school bands had that sound, a donkey with a cold). But who's coming home? she kept wondering. It seemed everyone was already there.

Lana was smiling again, thinking about Sam, that this would be funny to tell him tonight, how confused she'd been about homecoming, how actually absurd, if you really thought about it, the whole thing was. She'd called him collect from Megan's kitchen each night, after the household was asleep, laughing with him in a low voice, stretching the phone cord across darkness to the window so she could see the moon he was seeing too. They didn't stay on long, because it was late, and because these conversations in the dark left Lana vaguely guilty, as if she weren't giving Megan her full attention, as if she were betraying the friendship. She knew she wasn't. But after her years of dating in Chicago and almost marrying someone else, Sam was the first man Lana could talk to as she talked to Megan, in complete complicity. He was what she'd been hoping for all these years.

They were through Stamford now. This was Lana's least favorite part of the trip because at this point she was getting antsy from sitting, eager to get to her apartment, and also anxious that the weekend was ending. She pulled out her Month-At-A-Glance, not that she didn't know what was there, but to square herself.

Monday: the box was bare—she'd work on that book review.

Tuesday: five o'clock press conference/cocktails at Carnegie Hall. She'd eat enough hors d'oeuvres to stand for dinner. Then to Martha Graham performance with Dwight Davis. He was a dance critic, endlessly bugging her to write about ballet. "You know so much about it," he argued, and then he'd say over his shoulder, "anyone can write about theater." Maybe he's right, Lana thought, or maybe he just wants an intermission ally. New York dance critics were famously mean.

Wednesday: the new David Mamet play, one ticket—Lana never minded going to a show alone.

Thursday: Brooklyn Academy of Music—German Expressionism—a slog on the subway. Everyone loathed going to BAM.

Friday: three-thirty tea with Sylvie Moore, The Stanhope, and then meet Sam.

It wasn't the lightest week. And Lana wouldn't be seeing Sam 'til Friday, though she was going over tonight. Tea with

Sylvie would be just the right way to wind things down (as long as Sylvie didn't get broody, as she often did lately). That silvery green room looking out onto Fifth Avenue, those plush little couches that made you feel so proper, as if you were back in the 1950s (Sylvie, so tall and silvery herself—she really was too big for those couches). And tea followed by glasses of wine that floated you off into Friday night. Then she'd head home to her own little apartment, which, small as it was, she loved, and lie down for half an hour. It was one of her favorite things to do, especially on Friday before a date: lie down on her bed and watch the room darken, the fridge humming, the filtering gray. It was a stillness she always thought of as "pretheater," the hours between six and eight, a sensation both magical and sad that she felt only in Manhattan. It was, in a way, the New York equivalent of a screen door, something in-between, open and closed at once, slow and fast, the city eternally sifting. You had to push through, Lana thought—and now the train was underground and she could see her reflection in its thick window, her pageboy tucked behind her ears, her wide brown eyes.

"You don't blink very much," Sam once said.

He was right, she didn't. She might miss something.

Glue

Halfway through gluing the gimp on the Langham shade, Iris noticed she was losing the light. Autumn already. October. It was only three.

You couldn't rush gimp. It was the last step, the finish, and you couldn't stop in the middle. It was like fly-fishing, Iris thought, though she herself had never fly-fished, only watched her father do it, watched that smooth motion from the elbow as he practiced for a salmon-fishing trip he and her mother were taking in Scotland. You had to stay in the stream of it, hand and eye working a fine, lofting line, a kind of writing on air, all in the arm. Only with gimp it was all in the fingers.

To clothe a naked metal frame was a methodical process: every step left a raw edge to be covered up by the next step. Gimp—a trimming that Iris adored, heavier than ribbon, flatter than cord, as narrow as an eighth-inch but usually a quarter to three-eighths, and in countless colors and patterns—gimp covered the last raw edge. It should seem to have landed lightly, in flirtation or sympathy or love. To look that way, you had to lay it on deft and steady, no breaks. A light touch was the hardest touch of all.

Iris shifted the lamp shade a few degrees so that she would keep catching the light sideways. Iris had read that light coming through the side of your eye increases your control, puts you in an almost trance or Zen state. Iris wasn't sure what Zen was literally. You heard it everywhere, blithely applied to anything Eastern, and Iris guessed that most people were as blurry about it as she was.

"Zen," Iris said aloud. She took a deep breath, and continued with the gimp.

There were so many things to rush you in this world. The light going. The angle changing. As it had last month when she turned forty. Iris had vowed not to be frightened by that birthday, not to be humbled by the number that spells middle age. She went into it with her chin up, put on her best black silk, the cap-sleeve chemise dress, five years old but timeless, and took herself to the New York Philharmonic for Mahler's Ninth in an orchestra seat (where, uncrossing her legs to let some people by, she suddenly wondered is it my imagination or does my dress seem too short?). Then she met a few friends afterward for champagne, each relating how they dealt with forty, all agreeing that they felt "no change at all." But they, of course, were safely in couples.

Iris did feel a change. She felt a shift, felt the four o'clock aura of forty—the day not over, the evening at hand, that late-day sun so close in summer, so cool in winter, her new domain, four o'clock. She felt . . . not frightened, but pitches of panic. She began hemming down her skirts and dresses, the ones that could be hemmed down, to just below the knee. Iris was proud of her slim legs, but her knees didn't need to be blazing. This was more appropriate, soignée, more fitting of four o'clock. She calmed herself by living up to her word. She would be proud to be forty.

And if it wasn't the sun rushing you it was the designers who commissioned her lamp shades, quibbling, forever nibbling, at the due dates. Oh, can't we get it sooner? Oh, I know you said Friday, but I'll be in your neighborhood Tuesday. Oh Iris, why don't you train some assistants?

Because then these won't be Iris Originals, will they? And you won't want them.

The phone rang, three rings. Leashed to the lamp shade by gimp, Iris let her hand hover while she listened for the message.

"Ah-ris?"—sashay of Southern accent, it was Deena—"I bet you're in there doin' some swirl or twirl with pins in your mouth"—Iris never put pins in her mouth—"anyway our options tonight are *Elizabeth* at 8:05, about Queen Elizabeth when she was young. It's a prescreening and just down the street from you. So that'd be fun." Deena loved seeing things ahead of everyone else. "Or there's *Antz* at 7:50. It's not a Woody Allen movie but Woody's in it, or I should say, his voice is, so I need to see it sooner or later." Deena knew Woody Allen. She occasionally represented apartments he used as locations in his movies. "We'll decide when I get there. See ya at six."

Deena was the first friend Iris made when she moved back to New York, because Deena was the broker who helped her find her two-bedroom on Nineteenth Street, a block from Gramercy Park. Well, real estate brokers learned everything about you fast: that Iris had left a seven-year marriage in Phila-delphia; that her income was buttressed by a $20,000-a-year divorce settlement (all of it going toward the two-bedroom rent in the redbrick town house); that the second bedroom would be a workroom and therefore a tax write-off; that in this room Iris would work all day alone, keeping alive the dying art of the custom-made lamp shade.

Her Iris Originals were the most elegantly conceived, most imperiously executed silk lamp shades in New York City. And the highest priced. Which didn't mean Iris could make a lavish living with them. Even with the settlement checks, which Iris felt sheepish cashing but knew she needed (and could not bring herself to call "alimony," the word embarrassed her so), she was just scraping by, taking subways when she yearned to hail cabs. And yet the business, small and slow as it was, it was hers.

Iris had taught herself to cover shades during her marriage. It started when she took apart a very good, very old, lamp shade, a lark that filled the hours. She never dreamed this lark, then hobby, then freelance favor to friends in design, would be her meal ticket postmarriage. At the time, she was merely intrigued by the amount of craft that had gone into the water-stained creature she found in her mother-in-law's basement:

an old Biddle lamp shade, possibly from the 1940s. Despite the rips and spots you couldn't miss the sleek lines, like a Roman helmet. One by one the layers came off, a real struggle with the seam ripper, for though the silk was dead as dust, the thread, through decades of moisture and heat, had set, ossified. As each layer came away Iris saw what it had covered. She learned her art by going backward.

"I hope you're sure"—Deena had said at their first meeting, doubtful when Iris told of her divorce proceeding—"a good man is hard to find. *Any man* is hard to find." It wasn't the most helpful thing to hear. Especially coming from a single woman who was as lovely as Deena, with her deep dimples, her nuts-and-berries coloring, her look of a Southern belle raised in the woods (over a striped T-shirt she was wearing blue linen overalls, a boutique version of those roomy things toddlers wear—rompers!). She views me as competition, Iris had thought, and that's the last thing I need now. But Iris turned out to be wrong. Deena didn't compare herself to anyone, except maybe Audrey Hepburn in *Sabrina*—they had the same short bangs. As Deena later said, she immediately saw that Iris was "sorta formal," while Deena was a sprite. True, she had a knack for the double edge only another woman hears. "You look so *young*," she'd gush to Iris when they hadn't seen each other for a while, an annoying compliment, for it somehow implied that Iris usually looked old, and Iris knew she didn't. But Iris realized these comments weren't so much catty as uncontained, impulsive. And it was just these impulses that found Iris her perfect apartment with a key to Gramercy Park; just this gush that said ardently to Iris when Iris got behind schedule, "Let *me* be your assistant," even though Deena could hardly thread a needle. There were days when you couldn't put a price on such exuberance.

Iris and Deena spoke on the phone more than they actually saw each other, partly because Deena was often showing apartments well into early evening, and also because she didn't like to eat in restaurants as no stray additives were allowed into her mouth. Deena really did subsist on nuts and berries, brown rice and pea pods, things boiled, peeled, and steamed. Over dinner in Deena's Fifty-ninth Street apartment one night, the two of them picking at shrimp and chives with chopsticks, sipping spring water in blue glasses (blue, good for purification), Deena confessed that she hadn't felt well since a teen, that she had chronic fatigue or massive allergies or *something*—the doctors weren't sure what—hence the diet. Iris was stunned, not only because she never guessed her friend was suffering, but because Deena, in spite of this, had the energy of a running back. Her Rolodex never stopped spinning. Her rompers were always romping (velvet ones in winter, quite cute). She was eternally twenty. You'd never guess anything was wrong.

Now, six years into the friendship, Iris wasn't so sure the problem was entirely physical. She wondered if this phantom illness might be a way in which Deena protected herself, excused herself for still being single. After all, Deena was a year older than Iris and had never been married. That couldn't feel good. And despite the spinning Rolodex with the classy contacts (not to mention every well-to-do Southern couple in the city), there were no great ships on her horizon.

Only dinghies. And as everyone knows, by the time you turn forty, dinghies are demoralizing.

"I have to jump to the next level," Deena had recently confided to Iris, "so I get the megaproperties and the megamen. All men are rats, so I might as well marry a rich rat."

Not the most positive outlook, Iris had thought, but then what little Iris knew of Deena's childhood was that her father wasn't around much. Iris didn't pick up loneliness in Deena, just bright-eyed, deep-dimpled refusal to move on. Growing out of her bloom, she was stubbornly gripping the stems, holding on to the flower, a tension you could sometimes see in the sinews of her wrists, the fine cord in her neck as she noted who in a room was noticing her. Maybe that's what was stressing her body, the toll it took to stay a sprite. Anyway, tonight they would order in from Tang Tang on Twentieth Street. Deena purred over Tang Tang tofu. And the movie? Wild horses couldn't drag Iris to a cartoon about worker ants, not when she'd been slaving all day like a drone. A movie about the young queen of England would be much better for everyone's morale.

"We're going to *Elizabeth*," Iris said to the lamp shade. "And that's that."

It was time to cut the gimp. Eager, apprehensive, as she always was at the end, Iris measured three times before she cut. Then one last dab of glue—a dewdrop in a tiny cave of space Iris had left one step earlier—and the end of the gimp slipped in. She would hold it tight for five minutes.

The purist in Iris knew glue was not first choice, but stitching on the gimp was simply out of the question. Not only was sewing too time-consuming, easily adding two days to each medium-sized shade, it meant more needlework, and every stroke of the needle brought the risk of a pricked finger and blood on the shade. No one paid one thousand dollars—the starting price for an Iris Original (sconce shades were less)—for a smudged lamp shade. Which meant a week's work lost, and delivery and payment delayed. Glue was a compromise Iris was happy to make, and frankly, she enjoyed the gluing of the gimp. It was like licking the envelope and pressing it shut, the slant of her hand fused inside the folds, and held forever to the light.

Junk Journalism

Sylvie Moore never entered a room unnoticed. It was her height—five-ten in flats and bean stalk slim. And her hair, a fine frosty white that was like a gift from Mount Olympus (actually, it was a colorist's error, a chemical mistake that stunned the salon and transfigured Sylvie). A former photographers' model—"I was too klutzy for the runway"—Sylvie played herself down by folding forward, hovering in. She was eager to cavort with the mortals—"Lucky us," Sam said—finally to be heard after all that quiet in front of the camera. When she was feeling good about herself, pale face glowing as if a fever had just broken, lips glossed, hair snowy, Sylvie was amused by everything—and great fun to be with. When she wasn't feeling good about herself, which happened sometimes, what you noticed as she walked in the door was that pale brow, like a ghost ship in an ice floe. You had to coax her back. With Sylvie, it was Noël Coward or Ibsen—there was little in between.

Today was a good day, and Sylvie lit into the Stanhope Hotel's silver-green sun room, now set for tea. Lana tended to be there first, as Sylvie was always coming from another engagement, usually lunch downtown with another writer. Sometimes she even seemed to be coming straight from the night before— cocktails with a new editor—and still looked flush with the possibility of a big assignment, brimming with the flattery of being called rather than calling. As any magazine writer in Manhattan could tell you, there was nothing worse than having to peddle your wares. Cold calling was just that, Siberia. If editors weren't ready to look you up themselves, your only recourse was schmoozing, and there was an art to it. Sylvie had mastered the art.

"Hiiii," said Sylvie, swanning down for a peck on the cheek and then onto the plump upholstery as if onto a pond (hair smooth as a white wing, just long enough to pull back). She always seemed to float or perch or bob on furniture, not heavy enough to make a dent. Added to that was her habit of not always taking off her coat, as if she'd landed without entirely deciding to stay. Today, though, Sylvie shrugged out of a voluminous black mohair that might have belonged to Red Riding Hood's mother had she married the wolf. In a way, Sylvie did marry the wolf. She married Max—a partner at a Wall Street law firm, a prowler at parties known for his long list of conquests, both legal and lustful (pre-Sylvie, of course). Was it kept in his head or actually written down somewhere? No one knew, but Sylvie told Lana he once whispered the list in the heat of the moment, "and I know I shouldn't say this," she said laughing behind her hand, "but it was *really sexy.*"

Lana met Sylvie at a cocktail party full of lawyers. Sam, who had worked in Max's firm before jumping to a smaller one, was waved over by Max, who had Sylvie loose on his wrist like a silver bracelet. Her hair was boy-cut then, like swansdown. After the usual what-are-you-up-to shuffle, Max said, "My wife reviews things too." Lana blinked. People always got it wrong, stuck you with someone who just lived for The Arts but wasn't up on anything. What could Lana say to this glamour-puss? Sylvie flew in under Max's wing, and said, "Well, I'm not Mary McCarthy on Vladimir Nabokov but . . ." Lana grinned. A former model who had read Mary McCarthy's review of *Pale Fire?* Lana was hooked. She and Sylvie gabbed through three chardonnays, the whole party, Max and Sam finally pulling them apart as they lobbed their I'll-call-you's across a rain-slick street in SoHo.

"I hate that *Pale Fire* review," Lana said, swimmy with white wine in the cab to Sam's.

"Yeah, it's one of those smarty-pants pieces."

"But for Sylvie to even know about it, Sam, *that's something.*"

"I told you she was no dummy."

"She said I look like a young Diana Rigg, only shorter. *I love that!*"

"Shorter, younger, your face is rounder and your eyes are bigger. Other than that it's an amazing likeness."

"But Sam"—she loved saying his name—"isn't she too sophisticated for Max?"

"You're so naive. That woman is *Pale Fire* on two legs."

"To you too?"

"Me she scares. She's like a big tree that might fall on you. *Tim-ber!*"

Meeting for tea a week later, Sylvie and Lana had a great time. It seemed Sylvie had come to New York to be an actress (Sylvia Moore!) and failed her way into a successful (once her hair was white) modeling career, mostly commercials. She was the punk cowgirl in a long-running Coors ad, and the L'Oréal hair-color girl before they started using celebrities ("I lost even that job to other actresses!" she said in a huff, but smiling). All the while Sylvie never stopped reading scripts or going to shows, and when she married Max, she was ready to write.

"I'm working on a screenplay, though aren't we all."

I'm not, Lana had thought. Working on a screenplay was like playing the lottery. It wasn't real.

"But I've also published theater reviews"—Sylvie mentioned some small but respected literary journals—"and music stuff too. Believe it or not, I studied classical harp in high school." What was it with models and odd musical instruments? "Anyway, I think I'm ready to go for glossier magazines. Max keeps asking why I don't."

And here it was, a year later, open sesame for Sylvie. She was being published in mainstream magazines that Lana wouldn't bother to call, her own profile still so low. Lana wasn't jealous, exactly. She liked working at her own speed, giving each essay her all. She had faith she would eventually come into view. And she was objective about the fact that Sylvie had a huge leg up—her height and hair ("White Gold" on the

L'Oréal box)! Still, Lana couldn't help feeling, just the teensi-
est bit and Diana Rigg aside, like the little brown wren.

"You haven't been waiting long, have you?" Sylvie asked, digging into her tote bag for lip gloss. "I just hate it when I keep
people waiting. But the cab—we got caught behind a herd of
buses on Madison. A real jam!" She found the gloss, unscrewed
the lid, and with her long middle finger applied shine to her lips
without looking. Lana knew Sylvie would gloss two or three
more times. She looked luminous. And always, at first, her ice-
cap size was intimidating.

"Were you coming from home?" Lana asked. Sylvie and
Max lived in Murray Hill, a weirdly blank part of town, like the
blacked-out squares on a crossword puzzle. It was a dull question, but something to fill the lip-gloss pause.

"No," Sylvie said. Then she hinged forward as if with a
big secret. "I had lunch with an editor from *Vogue.* She saw
that piece I did for *New York* magazine and remembered me
from my modeling days. She called me. We're talking about a
contract."

The regular tea lady, a barrel in a ruffle, stood over the table.
They both looked up, Lana ordering Lapsang Souchong and
Sylvie, Earl Grey (she usually had English Breakfast).

"That's fantastic!" Lana said. "I was just reading *Vogue* last
week, on the train to Boston. I have to say I don't remember
any arts coverage. It would be perfect for you. And you'll get
one of those contributor's pictures!"

"I know," Sylvie agreed. "I haven't told Max yet. He's going
to think it's so cool. And Lana"—she lowered her voice—"the
money."

Lana lowered her voice too. "How much?"

"Freelance is three dollars a word. So just imagine what a contract might be."

Lana clapped her hand to her chest, pretend pain. Sylvie sat happy. The tea arrived. Earl Grey was poured first and the fragrance floated between them.

"You've never ordered Earl Grey before," Lana said.

"I know. But I just had it at lunch and loved it, so I thought I'd keep going."

"What do you love about it?" Lana asked. "Because the one time I tasted it I thought it was like an Englishman's eau de cologne. It's Prince Charles-y."

"But he's so *cute*," exclaimed Sylvie. "Don't you think? I can't believe you don't think he's cute! Those big ears and that sad face. Di was crazy, you know. Men are so vulnerable when they're married to madwomen. Like Edward Rochester. The wife in the tower." And then—one of her charms—she was laughing silently, her mouth closed in a cat-that-ate-the-canary curve.

Lana didn't find Prince Charles the least bit cute—his prim traditionalism, his cheating on Di. She could agree with Sylvie about the other stuff though, especially poor Rochester, one of Lana's first loves in literature. (And who couldn't identify with Jane Eyre? Well, maybe Sylvie couldn't.)

"Men do loathe scenes," Lana said, sounding to herself like a woman at tea at the Stanhope. "Any scene. Whether it's sending back your soup or having a nervous breakdown. Sam won't even hold my purse in public, if I need my hands free. Even for a second."

"Sam is so cute, in that bearish way of his."

"But to him, holding my purse, that's practically a scene. And now we're into third-generation feminism. My friend Megan, she says that girls today are confrontational, fully apprised of Their Rights. She watches it and feels sorry for the boys."

The finger sandwiches arrived.

"That would make such a great article," Sylvie said, biting a cucumber sandwich the size of a business card. "You should do that for someone. Why don't you call *GQ*? I know Lynn Johnson over there. We met at a party and then she called me. I could give you her number."

"I don't know." Lana held up an egg salad sandwich the size of a silver dollar, no, a quarter. "I think these egg salad sandwiches are getting smaller. But gender stuff, it's not my thing. That mix of sociology and anecdote, it's so predictable. Figuring out a performance, that's what I love."

The barrel came over and took their order, as always, for two glasses of chardonnay, to balance the tea.

"I love that too," Sylvie insisted. "But it doesn't pay. What's the most you can make writing for the niche publications? What did you get for that piece in *Opera News*, the one on Glinka?"

Glinka, it sounded so puny.

"Fifteen hundred words, fifteen hundred dollars. And it took me weeks, all that Russian research. By the way, Glinka used a lot of harps. At *Vogue*, though, you could really make a difference. Sylvie Moore—high fashion's voice of high culture."

"Well, they're not so interested in that. We discussed my writing about Hollywood. They like that I was an actress. The catch is, if I go with them I'll have to sign an exclusive. And lately, everyone's calling." Satisfied sip of white wine. It wasn't bragging, but it wasn't modest either. "So do I commit or keep dating?"

You commit to your writing, Lana thought. She had read Sylvie's early pieces. The voice was fresh, green, someone tall cutting across the field rather than taking the old road around. Direct! Which was always good. But lately Sylvie was striking poses in her writing, giving editors more of what they wanted—a former model's tart take on life. Her pieces were getting a little too "frankly" and "FYI" and *"entre nous."* Editors thought it "kicky." But Sylvie could be better than that.

"Maybe I should just sign the contract," Sylvie continued, "and hit the screenplay. It's just that I'm learning to love junk journalism. Quick and dirty. Pure positive reinforcement versus a pile of paper that may never see light."

"But it's not that simple," Lana replied. She took a sip (how nice to leave the office early on Friday) of chardonnay. The tea was cold and forgotten. "Most editors aren't quick, they're totally indecisive, as if each issue were their résumé. You'd think it was for-the-ages when most magazines are tossed in a week or a month."

Sylvie was giving Lana a look of quiet contemplation, which made Lana think uh-oh, I shouldn't have been so blunt. The ruffle, meanwhile, set down two more glasses of wine and whisked away scone crumbs. Sylvie forged on.

"I can't believe you don't like junk journalism! It's really fun.

The British are really good at it. They have no problem switching between high and low, literary and mass. It's all writing to them. Over here, people are a lot snobbier. 'Oh, I *only* do criticism, I *only* write fiction.' What about you? Wouldn't you write a celebrity profile?"

It wasn't something Lana had thought about. But she couldn't say that, Sylvie would take it as a slight.

"Well, no one's ever asked me to do one, but sure. If I liked the celebrity. Why not?"

To be honest though, it was hard for Lana to imagine herself writing "Gwyneth and I are sitting over steaming cups of tea when I ask Gwyneth what it's like to be Gwyneth . . ." Lana was much more at home with words like subconscious, iconographic, imperative. She was just now in the middle of her United Airlines book review, busily discussing Broadway dream ballets, how they were born from urban obsessions like surrealism and psychoanalysis and then got plopped into the middle of hick-town musicals like *Oklahoma!* and *Carousel*. It was fascinating—to Lana anyway.

"What are you working on now?" Sylvie switched gears, rapt and intimate. "You must have a lot of pieces going. Every editor must want you to write for them."

Lana, who had just this one piece going, was always a little lost in Sylvie's overstatements, but she took them in the spirit they were given.

"I'm reviewing this book on musicals set in small-town America, but the thing I'm really into is the dream ballets. They're so Freudian—but it's not like there were shrinks in Oklahoma in the 1800s. So you have these ballets that aren't nearly as innocent as the musicals they're in. I'm trying to sneak in a graph or two about that."

"But I can't believe you don't think those dream sequences are corny! They're so Salvador Dalí. A spiral staircase against a melting sky."

"Well they are a little dated," Lana said. "But I like that. They're so out there. And I love the way they push the action inward and forward at the same time." And what's so damn bad about Salvador Dalí, Lana wanted to ask, even though she was no great fan of his. There was something wrong when you felt driven to defend something or someone (Dalí!) you didn't even care about.

"I'm sure you'll do wonders with it." Sylvie picked the raspberry off a tiny tart. "You're just so good."

Lana was annoyed. It wasn't about whether she was good or not. If Sylvie was going to argue a point, then argue it. She contradicts me with this "I can't believe" and then backs out with a compliment. Sylvie was big on "I can't believe." It was a signature with her, another hyperbole like her hair and her height. Lana had her own phrases. She was always saying to Sam, "You have to admit that . . ." He'd say "Why do I have to admit that?" And she'd say, "Because you know I'm right." But that was a joke between them. Sylvie's "I can't believe" was slipperier, especially when she used it to question your opinion—"I can't *believe* you liked *Titanic*." It was like an end run. It got Sylvie around subjects, closing them off at the point they should be opening up, putting you instantly on the defensive. Why was every discussion short-sheeted? It was as if, for all her Valkyrieness, Sylvie was insecure.

"How's Max?"

It was an abrupt change of subject, but Lana thought they should get off shop talk. Sylvie ran a practiced hand over her hair. They were well into their second chardonnays.

"He wants a dog. He wants a place in Santa Fe. He suddenly says he wants children—he never wanted that before. He's burned-out at work but what else can he do? I mean, he lives for the kill."

"What kind of dog does he want?"

Sylvie laughed in deep conspiracy, as only wives laugh at their husbands behind their backs. "A Chihuahua!"

Lana shrieked.

"But is that even a dog? When I think of Max, I think, hmmm . . . a well-brushed boxer." Pondering Max, however, a man who managed to be both quick and bored, aloof and on-the-make, his nails buffed to a blush, his weekend jeans too snug for forty-five, Lana had to admit that a Chihuahua, all nervous and shivery, sounded just right, a little sniff at the norm.

"I know." Sylvie was shaking her head as if in explanation (there was no explanation).

A single glowing glass of chardonnay was placed between them to share. Sylvie poured half of it into Lana's glass, saying she'd have to dash in ten minutes. "We're meeting Mitch and Shane for dinner."

"Shaaaannnne," called Lana.

"We had brunch with them a while back. Their apartment was in *Elle Decor*." Sylvie looked wistful. "And so clean compared to apartments with kids. I don't want all that noise. And all that bright-colored plastic. I just want to do my writing. In New York. Isn't that what you want too?"

Slowly, almost apologetic, Lana said, "I do think I want children," even though there was no "think" about it. Of course she would have them, with Sam, that was her plan. But since she didn't know why Sylvie hadn't had kids, she didn't want to make a big deal out of it. Sylvie was only thirty-eight or thirty-nine, and yet they'd never discussed it. Their friendship was more about work.

"I just want to get good at junk journalism," Sylvie repeated.

Those flashy, cufflinky Js. They were getting to Lana. And the word junk—funk, sunk. There was a heavy downer built into "unk" words, a cement boot (kerplunk!). Where did Sylvie even get the phrase? Did she make it up?

"So I can make more money," Sylvie was saying, "and it really *is* fun to write." She stared into Lana's eyes as if opening a door to the next dimension. "You'd write for *Vogue*, wouldn't you? You'd take it if they offered you a contract."

Sylvie knew very well Lana didn't want the same things she did, so why was Sylvie pushing her into this corner? How much agreement did she need? How much cake and eat it too? It was ridiculous. Either that or the wine.

"Sylvie," she said, "they never would. They don't want my kind of writing."

"Oh. But they'll take mine, you mean."

Lana sat stung, slow, and Sylvie, injured, unleashed.

"You don't like *Vogue*. *You'd* never write for it. It isn't *serious* enough. I don't even know if you like my work. You never say. *What's with you anyway?*"

It was five-fifty. It was dusk outside and Sylvie had gone dusk as well. The electric chill, the stillness, it was a barometric pressure Lana knew from childhood, summer visits to cousins in southern Illinois—that vacuum after the tornado has passed, that tin tone in the air. Sylvie lurched into her black leather tote in search of what . . . lip gloss? Was she crying? Then a murmur, "so hard," and with that Sylvie straightened in her seat, face turned away, looking out the tea room's wide opening into the marble foyer, her cheek like marble too.

Lana felt she could hear Sylvie's silent index of accusation. I'm withholding. I'm dismissive and unsupportive. And yet it was Sylvie who had twisted Lana's words, willfully misunderstood her. She was now holding her wallet as if it might beam her up and away. Lana breathed in and leaned in, wronged herself.

"I didn't say anything against those magazines." She heard and hated her plaintive tone. "I think hiring you is a really smart move. I said that. And you know how talented I think you are."

But that was a finesse. Lana hadn't talked about Sylvie's writing lately. Because she couldn't think what to say that wouldn't sound like hedging—and everyone hears a hedge.

And even saying "you know how talented I think you are" seemed shifty, begging the question of what that talent was. But Sylvie softened enough to look back at Lana's hairline, to split the bill, to mock her own mood swing, to manage a tremulous smile. They walked a block together and then Sylvie was gone, a twist and pull of black mohair into the cavernous opening of a cab. Lana continued south on Fifth Avenue, dazed, playing the last scene over and over in her head, trying to feel better about things but still off balance, shaken. Night had fallen and store windows were lit up from within. "She made me *beseech*," Lana could hear herself telling Sam on the phone. She would make it funny at first. Later that night they would take it apart, and try to figure it out.

Thirty-five in Three Weeks

"What did Max say?"

Lana always liked it when Megan used the first names of New Yorkers she'd never met. It made Megan seem right in town.

"That Sylvie was out shopping but he'd give her my message. I said, I think she's been angry with me since our tea, and he said, I'll let you girls work that out."

"That means Sylvie *is* angry. He's doing that husband thing of not getting involved even though he's totally involved."

It was two Saturdays since the tea and Lana had left two shaggy-dog messages on Sylvie's machine with no calls returned. She had just called one last time and got Max.

"He was perfectly nice, but I could feel Sylvie was there"— Lana heard Megan take a sip of something—"*just looming.*

Maybe I should have said I'd take the contract, 'cause now I've lost a friend. Who will I go to tea with? Deena? She'd pull apart the finger sandwiches, checking for germs. I should have just given Sylvie what she wanted."

"But it's interesting you didn't."

"Well at the time I felt so . . . corralled. That feeling you get when giving is really giving in. She has all this going for her. Editors calling, on the verge of a glitzy contract, but that's not enough. No, I have to want it too, as if we're all trying out for the same team."

"Beautiful women need a lot of stroking."

"I know," Lana said, "save us from the insecurity of beautiful women." Megan was beautiful too, but she'd grown up with three brothers who laughed at lipstick, who made her play goalie in their backyard soccer games, who held her high when one of them accidentally kneed her in the chin and she took three stitches without crying. She was not insecure. In fact, she was practically slapstick, always looking for ways to crack Lana up.

"Tell me the turning point again."

"She said, 'You'd take a contract if they offered it, wouldn't you?' She asked it two different ways. And I said—being realistic, but also stubborn, I admit—they never would, they don't want my kind of writing. And she said in a flash, *Oh, but they'll take mine.*"

"Ouch."

"It was like whiplash. I was sputtering."

"I hate it when that happens."

"And then she said the other stuff I already told you. And now I feel guilty that I took a stand on something so small. But you know, at the time it didn't seem small. It seemed huge."

Lana could hear Megan exhale. Megan didn't smoke any-more, but sometimes she did on the phone. For some reason, people thought smoking on the phone didn't count.

"What's Sam's view?"

"He thinks it's classic female competition of the my-choice-is-better-than-your-choice variety. Add chardonnay and *blam*—hysterics."

"It seems more like a convergence. Sylvie's rising fast, but she's made a compromise, and you remind her of that. It doesn't help that you're younger. Also, when people get success too easily they don't trust it. They need more reinforcement, not less."

"Like those Hollywood actors with their entourages. One hit, overnight star, can't be alone."

"Right, the fame has no weight. It's empty. So they trash hotel rooms."

They were both laughing now.

"I tried so hard to be tactful."

"Lana, too much tact is condescending."

"But I'm not as high on her writing as I used to be."

"And you know she senses that."

"So—Can This Friendship Be Saved?"

"Is it worth saving is the question. You've already made three overtures. At our age most new friendships are short-term—you're just sharing the path for a while. It's not like you two were ever close."

"I know, but I feel sick that I let someone down. I don't let people down."

"You've given bad reviews, that's a letdown for someone—a lot of someones."

"Yeah but that's not personal. They put themselves out there to be judged."

"I think this is just Lana and Livia all over again. Her singing and you listening. You're too used to playing that supporting role. What's that line from *Gypsy*? The one the mother is always screeching?"

"Sing out, Louise."

"Right. Sing out, Lana. And go shopping. By the way, what do you want for your birthday?"

"What do you want for *your* birthday—yours comes first."

They were both turning thirty-five in November. Megan was a week older than Lana, which Lana never let her forget.

"Yikes," Megan said, "I gotta go. I only have an hour to work before picking up Elspeth from her play date. And then I have to clean up for tonight. Neighbors at seven o'clock. Drinks. In and out. So tell me quick, is everything else okay?"

Lana said yes and they hung up. It was one o'clock, a little too late to go shopping, the stores would be packed. She looked around her apartment which seemed to be waiting for something. Lana hated that, when the room was a pregnant pause.

Flopped on the bed she heard her own words again, I don't let people down. It sounded prideful. But Lana hadn't meant it that way. It's just she always knew she was stronger than other people, didn't need as much fawning and attention. She didn't know why this was, maybe it was genetic. Or maybe it had to do with the space between herself and the twins, as if she had two sets of parents, two skies overhead, and the whole green ground to herself. Or maybe it was the prime family commandment Thou Shalt Not Lie, Judge Burton's recurring theme ("jig-gle the truth," he'd say, "and it gets loose"). Lana had noticed that people who needed a lot of attention were often trying to be something they weren't.

Lana never forgot the teenage assessment of one of her best friends. "Lana, you're the sensible one." At the time it had stung. She wanted to be delicate, romantic, flamboyant. A flower, a comet, a poem. No. She was sensible like lace-up shoes. And yet she knew she was something other, more, than that. It was an instinct she had, an empathy. She'd looked up "sensible" in the dictionary. "Perceptible by the sense or the mind; able to feel or perceive." Well, yes, that did sound like her. So while her friends acted on their nerves, their fears, their whims, Lana made sensible a science. She matured into a gaze and a quiet; a gaze that took friends in whole—virtues, vanities—and a quiet in which she weighed their frailties so she'd know how careful to be. And so she would never expect more than they could give. She'd made sensible a form of omniscience. Megan's husband Jack, after reading one of Lana's reviews, understood her exactly. "It's like a dissection," he said, "but done with a feather."

Megan was right, though. Lana and Sylvie *had* come to a fork in the road. It was the swiftness in getting there that star-tled. And also, the sick feeling that someone doesn't like you anymore.

Lana got up and stared out her big casement window. It was an east view, blocked a little by the next building, but other-wise a good wedge of rooftops and open sky and two new sky-scrapers to the south. At night, this wedge was surprisingly dashing, all dark and starry like a Frank Sinatra song. Deena Pepper had found it for her, Deena, who'd been a friend ever since Lana's first weeks in Manhattan, when Lana learned how lucky she was that only half her salary was going towards rent.

"You're my second Chicago girl," Deena had cried. "Do you know Iris Biddle? She was the first. She's on Nineteenth Street, and a real artistic type like you."

Deena had wanted them all to meet but Lana had thought, enough Chicago. As much as she loved her home city, it had gotten so narrow, that long strip of Michigan Avenue, that oceanic lake glowering on one side—and her boyfriend pushing for marriage and that feeling narrow too.

Lana and Peter had dated languidly for almost two years. He was a banker at the Northern Trust, a slim handsome man who wore suits well and did his job with a sexy flourish, his fingers on the calculator like Van Cliburn on the keys. His true love, though, was the kitchen, where he chopped, diced, stirred big pots, steam in his face. It was fun watching someone chop. Soothing. His second love was restaurants, where he would guess the spices in the soups. He was a purist about food the way Lana was about art. To Peter, Megan's infamous chicken curry was just Uncalled For—he couldn't square the sugary look with the turbulent taste, the form at war with content. "It's like no curry I've ever seen," he said the night Megan made it for the four of them, right before she and Jack moved to Boston. "Which isn't to say it isn't good"—he was staring down at it in a kind of trance. "Can I see the recipe?" Megan handed it over and Peter studied it, squinting. "Is there something you do that's not written down?" Lana was almost wheezing trying to hold back laughter—the curry was as wonky as ever. Megan raised her hands helplessly; Jack chewed thoughtfully. Peter was polite, but in the cab home he couldn't stop talking about it. "That curry. It should be analyzed in a lab!" He kept mentioning it for days.

He was a nice nice guy, and in Chicago she never met anyone nicer. Often Lana would go to his apartment after a performance and he'd have set the table for late supper, sweet and romantic. He'd serve turkey or shrimp croquettes (Peter had a thing about croquettes), and they'd talk while she ate, charmed by these late-night tête-à-têtes, pleased with the way they were playing house, him serving her. They had the same values, and similar near-Northside upbringings, which can be very powerful after a run of dates with jerks. But the difference in their interests, which was exotic early on—a fun subject in itself—left an open question once the newness wore off. Peter had a limited tolerance for hole-in-the-wall theaters, the folding chairs, the burned coffee at intermission. He was ready for season tickets at elegant Orchestra Hall. And Lana, no matter how she tried to understand it, couldn't care about bank talk. Peter didn't discuss it much, but the little he did was soporific. Conversation shouldn't be this much work, Lana realized one night in a restaurant, when a handsome older couple at the next table were eating silently, passing the salt without words, and Lana was trying desperately for her and Peter not to be an early version of them. She found herself bringing up first times and funny evenings ("that curry") as a way to feel close, vivacious. And when he wanted to get engaged, she wanted, well, she felt excited by the embrace of it, felt the pull of the white dress, was nervous she was thirty and still single, and he was, after all, a catch. She kept looking at him hard, his Arrow-shirt profile, trying to feel a leap in her heart, trying not to feel that lurch of responsibility, trying to deny that dragging sensation ("this isn't what it should be"), that nagging refrain ("you have to break up with him"). The relationship itself was a croquette, too much flour and milk patted smooth into something it wasn't.

She didn't discuss the situation with her mother or Livia or even Megan, because if she did they'd be watching for her to do something and she wasn't ready yet to do something. She remembered Megan once saying—it made an impression— "Sometimes people get married because they don't know how to break up." Secretly, on weekends, Lana started scouring the help wanted section of *The New York Times*—under Editors. She started imagining a neat little New York office where she wielded a blue pencil, svelte in a new black suit; she pictured a nifty little apartment on the Upper West Side, and saw herself, notebook under her arm, marching down Broadway to Lincoln Center, the new critic in town. She stayed late in the office typing up cover letters, retailoring her résumé, photocopying her best clips, then sending these packets off like messages in bottles, knowing deep down it's never that easy, they'd get stranded on some desk.

But it was that easy. "Lana, get in here," her boss yelled from his corner office (the tyrant was only in Chicago one week a month, but usually in an okay mood because Chicago was so much nicer than New York and the offices so much bigger). The New York editor had quit in a huff—"It was a fucking Italian opera!" roared Lana's boss (he loved a fight)—and they needed to move someone up fast. It was the understudy getting to go on, *Morning Glory* all over, Lana's big chance. She didn't have to talk to Peter about love. She simply said, "I'm going to New York."

It was a good way to come to New York too, with a Broken Engagement behind her (though she didn't call it that, since it was never official). It felt worldly and brave. It gave Lana a mental edge on the competition, arriving breast high like Liberté with a torch, and in New York you needed every edge you could get, the city was stacked with attractive, accomplished women. Like those midtwenties, Hamptons-tanned assistants and associates on the rise, Lancôme eyes scanning the scene for Mr. Right. These girls were carefree, the seasonal, ritual round of Manhattan parties and cocktail dos stretching endlessly ahead. They drank oaky chardonnays and designer beer from bottles, were glossy and hungry, and their lack of concern was daunting.

On the other side of Lana were women in their forties, the ones who'd never married. Once perfect beauties, the babes of their day, they were now nuns to youth, taking the waters, the dance class, the vespers of vitamins A to Z. Long ago they'd arrived in New York with elf dew in their eyes, but now the storybook was closing and upkeep was all. It was twilight, the last chance to snag someone before their fifties set in, that gray sameness you couldn't help associating with Eisenhower, when these women were in kindergarten. And so they worked it hard, the Holly Golightly air of not caring. They worked it

too hard, afraid of the remainder bin! They were cautionary
tales and made Lana anxious.

But Lana also noticed that often these women, upon closer
inspection and behind the lipstick smile, were in some way out
of alignment. Deena Pepper was a perfect example. She was a
dynamo, one of those bright-eyed belles, soooo pretty, never
ruffled. But what you learned later was that Deena was like a
record with a warp: looked fine, but wasn't plumb, something
off, no one quite sure what. She was constantly changing doctors, trying to put a name to the problem. The latest theory:
she'd been dropped on her head as a baby.

And the women with Anger Issues—they were all around.
The tight little smile, the sharp little glance if you brushed
against them by accident, a glance both abused and abusing.
The whipping swivel in their theater seats if a coat touched
them or someone laughed too loud.

Sometimes Lana thought—and she knew this was totally
un-p.c.—that women really weren't meant to be single in their
forties. They got all twitchy. Lana wasn't going to get twitchy.
She knew the standard line in Manhattan, that women unmar-
ried in their forties didn't want to be married—they dated
unavailable men. Lana didn't know if this was true. Nothing
was that simple. She only knew she didn't want to be in that
situation.

When Lana met Sam, she couldn't believe he was available.
Looking back, she still couldn't believe it. It was at a book party
in one of those sprawling West End Avenue apartments that
seem to exist in an alternate universe, a world of butlers'
pantries and maids' rooms and—in this one—a library! It was

nothing like the East Side, Lana knew from glances at *Archi-tectural Digest*. This wasn't ritzy and gold-leafed, all interior decorated, money in masquerade. This was intellectual nir-vana. You walked in and wondered, Where Are The Trillings? Is Clement coming over? You knew you and your studio apart-ment were a Have Not, but it didn't matter because it was entirely possible that someday you'd Have This Too. Anyway, Lana was there with a sort-of date, Josh, a film critic she knew from Chicago, smart but too immature to take seriously. It was a crowded party and hard to move around. When Josh went looking for a bathroom, Lana positioned herself in a corner, to watch the scene and sip so-so chardonnay without getting jos-tled. She fixed on a guy against the far bookshelf who was with a perky blonde who looked too perky for him. The blonde grabbed drinks from a passing tray, urging an overfilled amber glass into his hand. Like a canary flitting around an honest brown Lab (he was trying to take a first sip without spilling), she grabbed his wrist and his drink splashed. She left, maybe to get a napkin, and he fished the maraschino cherry out of his glass, ate it, glanced around holding the red stem, then tucked it into his breast pocket. Such a guy thing to do, Lana thought. The girl returned and they moved off. Lana saw his tie was twisted in that guy-who-can't-get-his-tie-right way. Why is it so hard to meet the man you want to meet?

Josh found Lana and thirty minutes later, when they piled into the elevator with a bunch of people, she saw that the cherry guy and his date were in there too. It was quiet on the ride down because they were all too squeezed to talk. Lana looked through a keyhole of shoulders and saw he had slate blue eyes. When the door opened and he flattened to let the women pass, Lana nodded thank you and his look back made her heart bump. Josh, who'd shrugged out ahead of everyone, was waiting. Great, Lana thought, I'm with the date with no manners.

That would have been the end of it, just another ship passing in the night, and she'd never have known he was Sam. But a week later at Coliseum Books on Fifty-seventh Street, where she was skimming the latest critical journals—*The New Criterion, The New Republic, The New Leader*—who walked over but him! His face cracked into a smile that was new too. She hadn't seen it at the party.

"It's the girl in the elevator."

Lana was thrilled.

"And how are you?" she asked, madly thinking what to say next. "Did you have fun at the party?"

"It was nice to be in an apartment," he said. "Most book parties are in weird places these days, you know, alternate spaces. To show how hip the book is. This one felt—"

"Like the Trillings might have come!"

"Yeah," he nodded. "Sort of cozy, New York in the fifties."

He wasn't exactly handsome. His blue eyes were hard and his smile soft, and this discrepancy in his face was in his manner too. Lana felt he was shy, but game to be outgoing.

"But you weren't even born in the fifties," she said with delight.

That smile again. They started really talking then—told their names and jobs and each did some flips and somersaults, et cetera—and it seemed they hadn't stopped talking since.

When they went on their first date five days later, it was con-
firmed over brunch and a movie and cappuccinos and twenty-
five blocks of him walking her home (a first kiss on block ten,
and *Casablanca* kisses at her door) what Lana knew without
knowing at the party, that they were two halves of the same
whole. He was available because he had been keeping free for
her, just like she had kept free for him.

The sun had gone behind a cloud. Beyond the casement
window the sky was drab. Inside, Lana's white walls were
chalky, that standard landlord white. She had meant to paint
her apartment for three years now, but with her job, and freelance pieces, and curtain times, and Sam, there'd been no time
to pick a color let alone paint. And anyway, she was almost
never there during the day, even on the weekend, to see how
bored the apartment looked in daylight, a place left temporary
too long. At night the walls looked creamy.

Lana was always out of her apartment on Saturday afternoons. Since Saturday night was always a stay-over date at
Sam's, the afternoon was prelude to the date. Lana loved
shooting over to Saks, to check out the sales racks for something new to wear that night, so Sam wouldn't always be seeing
her in the same old thing. Sometimes on Saturday she'd dash
to a museum, usually the last day at a MoMA show or the Met,
where it was Lana and a cast of thousands, all of them getting
in under the wire, wishing they'd come sooner. And there
were always Saturday matinees—theater or ballet—though
Lana liked Saturday mats less and less. They made Lana feel
old, out of the flow of life, all those snapping purses and per-
fumed matrons. Sam, on the other hand, was perfectly happy

in matinees or movies during the day, like a bachelor bear finding a convenient cave.

Drab outside, drab in. I could drop off dry cleaning and
then browse Fifty-seventh Street, Lana thought, seated on her
orange loveseat as if she'd taken root. What she really wanted
to do was call Sam, but she never did on Saturday afternoons.
It was sort of a rule she'd made. To keep alive the image of her
independence. So she'd be sassy and fresh for Saturday night,
not the boring old blather he just got off the phone with.

I could go to the hardware store and get a new stopper for
the sink, Lana thought, not budging. You really felt single when
you were in alone on a Saturday afternoon. And soon she'd be
thirty-five. She wouldn't be 25–34 anymore on surveys. She be
35–44. And wasn't thirty-five the age for amniocentesis? And
mammograms?

Oh Sam, she thought, why are you so slow?!

That was the other reason Sam had been available. He was
totally set in his ways. Sam was a loner by nature, a reader and
shutterbug. He was a very good lawyer, specializing in artistic
copyright infringement, but one of those wan lawyers who'd
rather be doing something else, in Sam's case, tooling with his
camera collection. He had his own settled state on East
Twelfth Street, a bookish one-bedroom with a cat, Spiffy. Lana
had no doubt that Sam loved her. She believed he didn't want
to lose her—he told her so sometimes, whispering it as she fell
asleep. But she also knew that his solitary habits were a form
of thick winter coat, to keep out cold and pain. He was like
Jane Eyre's Rochester, sensitive, but covering it up with gruff-
ness. His girlfriend history, as much as Lana could get out of
him, was that they pushed too soon, he resisted, they walked

away thinking him unmarriageable. Lana, if she said so herself, had been brilliantly disciplined in her handling of Sam. Her ability not to expect too much, her patience (she'd never once uttered the M-word), had made Sam happy and easy. But now maybe he was *too* easy with things. Lana saw they were coming to their own fork in the road.

We've been dating a year and a half, she thought. Next May will be two years. That's my deadline. She wouldn't make it marriage, that would flip him out. The next step, and in a way the much bigger step, would be living together. It would show him he could do it. There it was: move in or move on.

Lana had been listening to a set of expensive negotiation tapes that was circuiting her office. They were meant to help the staff deal better with difficult clients, but Lana listened to them with a different application in mind. These were time-honored rules of the game. The goal was win-win; the ethics, luminous common sense. And Lana loved the stern refrain that drummed through the tape like a cold conscience: You cannot win a negotiation if you are unwilling, in the parlance of the tapes, to walk away from the table.

Move in or move on. It wasn't that Lana wanted to give Sam an ultimatum, but she also didn't want to be strung along, waiting like Penelope for Odysseus. Sam would have to make a choice and the less wiggle room the better—for both of them. According to the tapes, to win it all you had to be willing to lose it all. Sam was everything to her, but if he couldn't commit . . . better find out sooner than later. Right?

But what if he said no?

Just thinking it—Life Without Sam—Lana teared up a little, the room wobbling. She saw herself newly alone at thirty-

five, back in the boat with the other menless, starting from
scratch with older dates who had that much more bitterness
under their belts. And all those city sidewalks leading nowhere
(or to neurosis), Saturday afternoons a prelude to nothing,
Sunday mornings by yourself with a bagel, and of course, the
second death when she eventually saw Sam with someone
else. Lana let herself feel lost.

But she couldn't be afraid. She wasn't ready yet, but she had
to get ready, steel herself, practice what she'd do if he said no,
get used to the possibility of pain, like holding her hand over a
candle flame. It would be like a dream ballet—she'd dance it
in her head until she mastered every leap and pause. How she
would put her desire on the line, how she would smile above
her broken heart, how she was sorry they couldn't go forward
together, how she would turn away and not look back, the
simple dignity of her good-bye. In a few months they would
play the scene for real. When Lana was ready to risk it all. Sam
wouldn't let her walk away, would he?

Standing Room

Iris hadn't asked for this assignment. She was perfectly content to finish one lamp shade and begin the next, her silk beauties doted on and feather-dusted by Park Avenue grande dames and Amster Yard dandies. There was sometimes a six-month waiting list for a custom-made Iris: she could only make one per week (sconce shades were faster), and a limit of four per client per year (eight for sconce shades). So what was Iris herself doing in a line?

As usual, helping Deena with one of her hare-brained schemes. Except this one wasn't so hare-brained. And it wasn't entirely Deena's. One of Deena's newest friends, a young woman she'd found an apartment for on Twenty-sixth Street, the flower district, was starting up a new magazine called *Petunia*—art, culture, fashion, funk, the usual. Wanting to make a splash with her first fashion pages, this gal decided to ask three "artistic women" to judge some shows during Fashion Week. It was an angle.

"It was actually my idea," Deena said on the phone, "but at some point it became her idea. So okay, whatever. But I'm gettin' mine back by havin' her use my friends!"

Iris Biddle was one of the names Deena spun out of her Rolodex ("She never heard of you," Deena gushed, "but I assured her that those who know, know you.") Would Iris, the *Petunia* girl asked—the enigmatic Iris of elite lamp shade fame—go to some shows in Bryant Park and then weigh in?

Well, why not? Iris had been feeling cooped up lately. Nobody knew what trouble it was to make such impeccable lamp shades—the many tiny slips that could ruin a day's work and a hunk of costly silk. No one knew how stressful these big-ticket commissions were, the concentration required as you strong-armed the fabric into place, getting the foundation right. Iris put music on in the morning—Mozart for his glorious reason, Bach because he picked up the pace—they inspired her, helped her to begin. But she preferred to work afternoons in silence, sun shafting through the blinds as she positioned silk on the frame on the bias, pinned it, then commenced repinning, pulling the silk tighter, first along the lines of a "+," then outward in an "x," then once again, tighter still, then again, the grain giving until it could give no more, all give radiating from the center until it was its own music—"beauty like a tightened bow"—and you could bounce a dime off it. Iris would not put her name to a loose lamp shade. She liked to see line, she liked clean fields of silk, and light not having to fight through fussy folds. The most outrageous shade she'd ever made—a fantastic chinoiserie for a flush financier in Paris, an elaborate pagoda of oyster silk, moss green gimp, and turquoise tassels (three weeks it took; the bill four thousand dollars)—even this was a model of swirling, curling quiet. By the end of a good day's work, Iris felt she was climbing out of a rabbit hole. By the end of the week she was dying to talk. So yes, she told the *Petunia* girl, she'd be delighted to go to some shows, but she could only spare two days.

Iris had imagined herself strolling into the salon, or the tent—that's where the designers showed these days, in big circus tents behind the library at Forty-second Street—with a sharp new haircut. Or maybe she'd do a marcel wave; she'd always wanted to and it *would* suit her. She'd stroll in with her neat head and nice posture—"Who's that woman?" everyone would wonder—and take her front-row seat. Well, probably not front row, since Iris knew enough to know that these were reserved for fashion gurus and the latest celebrities. Maybe third row.

But no one, not Deena or the *Petunia* girl, had prepared her for the crush at the entrance, the hungry eyes of struggling twentysomethings (their nails painted bug brown) desperate to push in. Or the insolent eyes of their more polished peers, whose posh jobs floated them in. Or the royal air and trademark hair of women in their forties who'd been doing this for decades and walked in surrounded by their staff, their girls— queen bees tended by clones in Gucci stilettos.

And no one told Iris that getting to your seat was like running the gauntlet, trying not to trip on extension cords taped to the floor, and having to climb gym bleachers in heels. The gals in headsets would look at Iris's invitation and point upward without interest. It was Everest every time, with Iris in the eighth row—the last—at every show. Up there with the unpopular, she'd think. So this is the fashion press. Iris had never seen so much hair pulled back randomly in rubber bands, so many separates that wrenched and revealed private swells and black bra straps. The buyers, who sat on the other side of the runway, sleek in Armani and Bill Blass, were less tribal, more groomed, more Iris's cup of tea.

At the first show Iris attended the designer seemed to be making ensembles for rich hippies, though Iris wasn't sure she could use the word "ensemble" since nothing actually matched. It was like Woodstock in Disneyland—Peter Max colors, fringed hip huggers, lots of drawstrings and belly buttons. It's pot party chic, Iris thought. But for who?

If only the designer had gone back one more decade, back to Dior and Balenciaga. Iris had never worn their clothes—she was much too young for that—but she had studied their work in books, and could identify with the presixties notion of correctness. And also correction. Bodies were not perfect and they were not trustworthy, the id and all that. The French masters of seam weren't interested in peekaboo and belly buttons. They sewed one into a world of order and aspiration. Made one airtight and contained. But also, paradoxically, perched for flight, chin lifted.

"The contradiction in every act, The infinite task of the human heart."

Iris loved this line from Delmore Schwartz, from her poetry-reading days in her truth-and-beauty twenties. She didn't quite understand it back then, but thought she understood it now. The sadness mixed in with happiness. The something exquisite you found in sorrow. It was a feeling she couldn't quite keep out of her lamp shades, which seemed to offer her their bones (a steel frame) in return for a soul (a cast of light). Every lamp shade was a different life, a piece of the past. Rittenhouse Square circa 1910. London between the wars. Nancy Mitford's Paris sitting room. It had been the formidable Sister Parish, late headmistress of New York decorating, who first saw what Iris was doing, and with a major order gave the business such a boost. "You're overly poetic," she said, "but absolutely correct. That tension is your power. Don't lose it."

Power, Iris sighed, standing in a lumpy line a long way from the entrance to the Calvin Klein show.

"I'm sorry," the young woman in black seated at the table draped in white had said when Iris asked for her seat assignment. "You're not on the list but if you'd like to get in line you might be able to stand."

Stand?! Iris had looked into the shallow waters of the blue eyes below her, and for a second was going to say, "but I'm here for *Petunia* magazine," and then thought: Who cares about *Petunia?* Who's *heard* of *Petunia?*

"Standing?" Iris repeated.

"Over there," the girl directed, her sympathy getting brittle as she turned to the next victim.

"Over there" was where Iris was now, in a group of outcasts waiting for a train to nowhere. Iris was torn between a sense of duty—she'd said she'd go to this show—and a sense of self: I

Don't Stand. She was forty, for heaven's sake. She'd done standing room in her twenties at the Met, Covent Garden, the Staatsoper in Vienna. She would have stood almost *anywhere* for the conductor Carlo Maria Giulini, because of that fine craggy profile on his album covers and the sweep of his Brahms symphonies. But for Calvin Klein, an underwear maker?

Standing room, Iris contemplated. It was a quite a ways from the Biddle box at the Philadelphia Orchestra, the Biddle table at the annual Hunt Ball. None of that mattered of course—a square box, a round table—but there was no denying it was exciting at the time, to know there was a place for you whether you wanted it or not. Anyway, it was borrowed time. Iris's husband was the Biddle with a PhD in neuropharmacology who quit science cold, railing against the old-boy politics of the NIH, raiding his trust for a pipe dream in Tanzania. Brilliant Erich Biddle, in love with logic, who could find airtight reasons for not doing, not staying, not loving—the man who once said he'd never let her go.

Iris had joined the huddled masses behind the nylon cord with as much dignity as she could muster. As she passed those unhappy faces on her endless walk to the end of the line (well it seemed endless, though there were only about eight people so far), she tried to rise above. Why should it pain her to be stuck in this line? This wasn't her world. She hadn't earned a place in its hierarchy. Still, she was going to wring Deena's neck.

There was a certain solace in knowing she looked good, slim and trim in her vintage Norell flyaway jacket with the up-

turned collar and long cigarette skirt, her glossy black alligator
bag and Chanel slingbacks. Not quite *in* fashion—rather, she
hoped, beyond it. Her friends were always amazed at the looks
she came up with, the little twists on the norm that made her
stand out ("and on her budget," they probably said to each
other). But maybe standing out in the standing-room line
wasn't the best idea. For as the queen bees started to breeze
past, their entourages pleased and protective, Iris began to feel
conspicuous. She wasn't a Parsons kid pushing in for love or a
fashion queen trying to start his own newsletter. Iris was obviously someone. "But who?" those speedy glances wondered in
the seconds before they dismissed her elegant image from
their minds. If she were Someone she wouldn't be Standing.

This isn't fun, thought Iris, as she watched the women
who ruled the glossies make their late and unapologetic
entrances. There was that small, spidery creature from *Vogue*
who hunched her bony shoulders as if against ancient winds,
who styled her hair like the Sphinx and wore sunglasses into
the darkened tent as if begging for a bulb. Iris would have
liked to stick one in her mouth.

Next came one of those keepers of Diana Vreeland's flame.
This woman brushed her black hair back and away, and wore a
sort of boiled wool kimono that created a stiff circle of space
around her. She'd better watch the boiled wool, Iris thought,
it's a bit witches of *Macbeth*.

"There's the editor of *Q+A* magazine," said the fashion
queen standing next to Iris, nodding toward a pudgy gal striding by. He started laughing. "Doesn't she know grunge is over?"

In her large aviator glasses, chartreuse suede Hush Puppies, and a very hairy mohair sweater from the fifties she looked like the militant coed everyone avoided in the dorm lounge. Except now she had clout. "She's Lucy and Pig-Pen," Iris whispered back, "all in one!"

Enough, thought Iris. If something doesn't give in five minutes I'm leaving. And then she saw that it was too late: her worst nightmare was twenty yards off.

Iris and Victoria Pines were not exactly enemies. No, they were sorority sisters who had disapproved of each other on sight. Victoria had picked her career track—radio, TV, film— and, beginning with a postgrad internship, tucked into it as if it were a prize truffle (in the sorority's *Winnie-the-Pooh* rush skit, Vicki had cornered the role of Piglet for three years running, giggling all the way). Iris pursued English literature with a minor in decorative arts, wrote an award-winning senior thesis on chandeliers, and graduated jobless.

Victoria climbed the anchor-person ladder, springboarding from the Pittsburgh stint to a national "animal channel" in New England, where she grew very popular covering pet rescues, environmental battles, and the plights and politics of farm animals. Meanwhile Iris had surfaced as a junior specialist at Christie's, dating lovely older men with lovely older oil paintings, forging through late Tolstoy and early Edith Wharton, and then marrying dashing, eligible, enviable Erich (they first flirted over an antique microscope he thought he might bid on) and falling into the side pocket that is Philadelphia.

Victoria moved to New York, and married a portly, rich Wall Street broker. Iris moved back to New York—divorced—just in time to witness Victoria's latest metamorphosis: she was now the city's number one arts anchor.

The arts! This from the gal who had mocked Iris's class on Nietzsche, laughing loudly about the great job prospects in Japanese printmaking (Ni-Chi?). Vicki had no feeling for the creative, but she had rude drive and could ask any question without blanching. She'd asked Baryshnikov if his perfume smelled like him pre- or postperformance? She'd asked Jessye Norman, heading into the Metropolitan Opera, if it really took great weight to support a great voice? It turned out that Victoria had a huge following among the arts-antagonistic of the 1990s, that segment of the population who knew the arts were important but hated the special status of artists, and liked to see them brought down, humbled for their high profiles.

Iris couldn't countenance Vicki, and wondered why it hadn't occurred to her that their paths might cross here. But Iris refused to turn her face, or worse, to scrunch down behind the other standees. She accepted fate—another way in which she knew she was old-fashioned. She took Vicki's stare square in the eyes, felt the Concord force of Vicki's decision to steer straight toward her, camera guys hustling along, attached by black coils like a life-support system. Vicki stopped about five feet away, put her hand scoutlike over her eyes and, leaning forward as if looking into a dark cave, called, "I-ris?"

Oh the irreverence, Iris thought, knowing she now had to smile and respond (if she were a good sorority girl she'd have shrieked into Vicki's arms).

"Vi-cki," she pronounced as if she wasn't in this awful line but floating in from a rose garden.

Vicki swept over, taking over. "I don't know what you're doing here at Calvin's." She ran her eyes up and down Iris. "By the way, you look fabulous. But no sorority sister of mine is going to stand in this line. They're holding the show for me, so come on."

Iris shook her head. "You hurry on in," she said, then turned her voice down to a whisper, "I can't leave these people now. We've been waiting together and it wouldn't be fair."

And really, it wouldn't be right, they'd stood together just too long. The newsletter guy looked at her as if she were nuts.

"Iris. What planet are you on? It's not about fair. It's about getting in. But if you don't want to, suit yourself. Anyway," she threatened as she edged off, her men pulling like hounds, "you'd better start coming to chapter meetings. The next one's at Amy's and I'm going to have her call you."

And with that Vicki and company hustled toward the tent, Iris and the line watching them recede as the faux-solicitous voice of Calvin's henchgirl caught them from the side, telling them that standing room was filled (filled? with who? not one of them had left the line!). They were welcome to watch the show on the monitor in the corridor.

Watch TV? Standing in a makeshift corridor?

It was too much. While the girl deflected questions from the angry unbudging line Iris headed out, walking as tall as possible, vowing silent revenge on Calvin Klein, that minimalist panty-preneur. For *this,* she thought, I interrupted work on the Kravis shade, pinned and waiting to be stitched. And now it was rush hour at Grand Central Station, a battle for every cab—she'd have to take a lumbering bus down Lex. Just endless. One of those endless days with endless indignities. *That's what you get for going out . . .*

It was a ridiculous thought: not going out. Iris knew today

would be ripe for retelling, that sad standing line, those pushy
girls. Everyone had days like this. All the same she was hungry
to get home. In her living room with the leafy trees outside
she'd be fine, slip free, shoes off, have a bath. Then she'd make
herself a big martini, quiveringly cold. It was Friday after all.
Martinis were the Atlantic Ocean, summer parties, midnight
dips. They were stars dissolving in a black night sky, another
life. "Hypothermia in a glass," her husband had called them
happily at first. She liked that sensation, rationed it, the blue
freeze in small sips. Remembering, forgetting. The clarity, the
drift.

Aisle Seat

Lana had C-2. A great seat, right on the aisle, first ring. She had never been up in the first ring before, that low and airy berth of balcony, and she couldn't help feeling pleased. She was a critic now, a dance critic. Not exactly what she had pictured, but you never knew what life had in store. Lana was reviewing for a legendary—well, once legendary, now a trifle left behind—academic quarterly. They wanted four essays a year. Not thumbs-up-thumbs-down, not I-laughed-I-cried, but pieces with ideas.

"But what if I can't come up with any ideas?" Lana wailed to Sam when she told him the good news.

"You can and you will," he said. On their next date he presented her with a red Waterman pen, to commemorate her new status. The note said, "Go for blood—love, Sam."

Now where was Dwight Davis? They had synchronized their watches earlier in the day, planning to meet here in the lobby. Lana staked out a place at the top of the stairs, on the side where the Jasper Johns sat, a huge gray grid of numbers o through 9. From there she watched ranch minks and herringbones stream in, mufflers unwinding and bumpy embraces of hello. She wondered who would be seated beside her in C-4. The established critics, the ones attached to the gritty dailies, the glossy weeklies, they got pairs. They never wondered who they'd be next to.

C'est la vie, thought Lana. Her aisle seat in the first ring was more than enough. The dance critics of New York were the best in the world and she was suddenly among them. Scary if you thought about it. So where was Dwight? If it weren't for him she wouldn't even be doing this. He'd nagged and nagged her to write about dance. He said, "You actually took ballet. You know the five positions. You can *do* an arabesque. None of these other gnomes—excuse me, Our Esteemed Colleagues—have sweated at the barre."

"But Dwight," Lana countered, "I was the girl whose underpants bunched."

He'd hooted—Dwight's distinctive sound—part laugh, part war cry. With Dwight, everything was war.

"You didn't figure out that dancers don't wear undies?" He was shaking his head in disbelief.

"Yes I figured it out. But I was shy. I knew those other girls were better than me. My undies were my security blanket."

The day Lana showed Dwight her in-flight piece—which he insisted on reading then and there, in the last remaining fried-eggs dive near Lincoln Center—when he got to the graphs about dream ballets, he just dropped his jaw ("catching flies" Livia always called that) and said, "Shit." More head shaking. "I'm slavin' away devoting my life to dance and you just toss this off? For United-fucking-Airlines?!" Lana loved that kind of compliment, when the person wasn't afraid of your talent, when they thought it was cool. He then told her the name of an editor at a quarterly looking for a dance person. "Call tomorrow."

"But why aren't you going for the job?" Lana asked, skeptical. A compliment was one thing, but if Dwight had his way he'd write every column in the city.

"They ran a piece trashing Truman Capote and I can't deal with that."

Lana took this with a grain of salt—you never got the whole story with Dwight.

"But with you in there," he said, "at least it would be one of us."

Lana sent clips in early December, they took her to lunch in early January ("We don't pay much, but we do nice restaurants once in a while"). It was mostly chit-chat and tactical name-dropping—not the rich and famous, but names of competitive journals, literary controversies. Lana guessed she passed because over coffee they suggested "twenty-five hundred words, New York City Ballet, winter season," and it was done. When Lana told Dwight, he said, "Too bad you can't start with a hatchet job on *Nutcracker.*"

"I thought you loved *Nutcracker.*"

"Act Two I do, the dream. But Act One should be nuked.

Boys with drums, girls with dolls—it's Ozzie and Harriet in Düsseldorf. The horror, the horror."

A typical Dwight point of view.

He loved classicism but hated conservatism, he loved beauty but hated tradition. This made for much internal tension. You could see it in his wardrobe. He dressed in a style Lana thought of as punk good ol' boy, seersucker suits in summer with just a T-shirt underneath—and a dangle earring of a skull. Or like now, pushing through the big glass doors of the State Theater, long stick legs in skinny black jeans, his short black bomber jacket opening on a Brooks Brothers' buttondown and Tweety Pie bow tie. In winter, Dwight always seemed to be wearing one layer less than necessary (standing in line to get his press ticket, his face looked freezing). But even in summer he had a sharp-nosed, hungry look—maybe because he was always recently fired and near eviction due to the fact that he saw Mendacity Everywhere and couldn't Maintain Relationships. Dwight was Cajun, so he was a Southern gay cliché with a twist, his aesthetics all peppered up, his refinement pan-fried. To him, Stanley Kowalski was the tragic hero of *Streetcar*. And the problems between Rhett and Scarlett? Obviously they were both tops (and Ashley was a classic bottom). Dwight was fun 'cause he kept you hopping.

They were both young critics and had a bond in that. They could disagree with each other and not take it personally, perhaps because they were so different, so *not* in competition. Lana liked Dwight's hunger, his blind love of ballet and his outrageous opinions. She was delighted by the energy of his ambition, so naked, so different from her own. Where she was steady, and sometimes felt she hid in steadiness, not trusting things that happened too fast, Dwight reached boldly, lustily, sometimes questionably. Was that corps boy really a fine technician or did he simply turn Dwight on? Did Dwight really like the new ballet, or did he just want entrée into the director's inner circle? He wasn't 100 percent trustworthy—but Lana loved him. And if you called him on the corps boy, he'd laugh a low sneak's laugh, puff deep on his cigarette, and say "fuck you" in soft smoky assent.

"Dwight!" Lana pressed her cheek to his.

"Where are you sitting?"

"C-2," she said trying not to sound overpleased. "What about you?"

"B-3."

Evens were on the right, odds on the left, and for some reason, the right was better.

The chimes were ringing, but it was the first call. Lana and Dwight stayed where they were, watching the scene. When Dwight saw colleagues he liked, he'd nod or wave and then explain who they were to Lana. Even more, he enjoyed seeing people he couldn't stand. Then he'd cackle and say—in the same way you'd say *pssst*—"there's so-and-so, the idiot critic at such-and-such." Lana, a little draggy from working all day, was trying to decide whether to get a fast cappuccino when Dwight said sidearm, "Her highness is here." Even Lana knew that could only be one person. Cassandra Rogers was coming through the glass doors, complete with aura and three acolytes.

Was it otherworldly drift or state procession that described the bubble of self-absorption in which Miss Rogers moved? She walked with geishalike quiet, small steps in suede snow boots. You expected to see her in robes and scarves, but here she was in a long down-filled coat, padded like a piano. Her prim mouth was still, her eyes straight ahead. People stayed out of her path, never approaching directly, sidling in to pay homage *diminuendo*.

Miss Rogers. She insisted on Miss, not Ms., which she thought an affront to the language (she was *not* a manuscript!). She was in her sixties and had been writing from on high for twenty years. Her career had begun in the heat of discovery: What is this thing called ballet? Each essay was a romance, awaited by a readership that was not only discovering dance, but discovering Cassandra, "the chastity," one fan fawned, "of her prose." She blazed with industry, covered her subject—so long ghettoized as the art of girls and gays—in glory. Those were the days of Mikhail Baryshnikov and Gelsey Kirkland, Suzanne Farrell and that lord of choreography, George Balanchine. Then the end began, the crucifix and the guillotine: Balanchine died, favorite dancers aged, and those disfavored got the blade edge of Cassandra's steel sentences. And then came apotheosis. She rose above her subject, cooled, grayed, wondered Whither Ballet? The writing shaded into dismay, a faded wrist pressed against her forehead: What is to be done? She had minions and protégés, handmaidens of both genders who served in the Temple of Cassandra, sifting the ashes, preaching the gospel of Rogers in their own reviews and think pieces. They were called Cassettes.

Dwight was humming "It's a beautiful day in the neighbor-hood" and Lana was feeling giddy. Cassandra's judgmental presence, that zone of frozen reserve, seemed to alter the atmospheric balance, to set egos jostling. That's what power did in New York. Any power. Lana had felt it at Carnegie Hall, when Arthur Levitt Jr., head of the SEC, walked in. She felt it at the Metropolitan Opera, when Arnold Schwarzenegger and Maria Shriver (weird but true) walked in. And she felt it now—the hiss and crackle here in Miss Rogers' Neighborhood—and so did Dwight. He was bringing his tune up-tempo as Cassandra passed out of earshot.

"Don't you think she gets tired," Lana said, "holding up the temple with her head?"

"Embalmed in Bitterness," Dwight intoned. He had a poet's way with words sometimes.

"So where do we meet at intermission?"

"You mean what corner of downtown Beirut?"

Dwight was always joking about ballet intermissions. Machiavelli Live!, he called them. *"Thunderball,"* he said. "The sharks in the water." He wanted to write a book, Every-thing I Know About Life, I Learned in Intermission.

"Not the acro-Fats." That's what Dwight called the Nadel-man sculpture upstairs, gargantuan girls carved from lard (actually, white marble). There was a pair on each side of the first ring promenade, and depending on your critical clique, you met at one, the acrobats, or the other, the nudes.

"The nudes," he reiterated, "but I'm gonna need a smoke."

With the last bell they shot upstairs, he went left and she went right. Going to her seat, taking slow-boat steps down the crowded aisle, Lana saw a head of silvery black hair in C-4. It was Fernanda Levine.

Before sitting down Lana set her purse under her seat, feeling that taking your seat on the aisle required some bit of preparation. Fernanda Levine glanced up, then away, unimpressed. Lana knew what Fernanda was thinking—Why does *she* get the aisle? Fernanda edited her own dance magazine, a quarterly called *Divertissements*. Since there were no ads in the magazine, Fernanda and her writers could say whatever they wanted. Which they did. *"D,"* as insiders dubbed it, was rigorous, intelligent, witty, sarcastic, extremely contrarian. In short, it was like Fernanda herself, whom Lana had watched from a distance (Fernanda up close was unnerving). Still, Lana would have liked to nod a hello, but getting no encouragement, she busied herself with her notebook and new red pen and eventually the lights came down on the first ballet, an old standby.

When it was over, Lana popped up fast as critics do and scooted up the aisle before everyone else spilled out. Dwight was fast too, already at the bar buying himself a bourbon.

"Oh, did you want something?" he asked, an absentminded professor all of a sudden.

Lana knew Dwight didn't have money to treat. She didn't begin to expect it.

"I'll have a seltzer water," she said to the bartender. "Dwight, you go get us a spot, the hordes will be here any second."

And they were. Getting through the intermission crowd, especially with a drink in your hand, was like moving through a maze. When Lana got to Dwight he'd already hooked up with some other balletomanes. Her arrival, however, put an

imperceptible damper on things and they soon left, but gracefully. Gay men could be very graceful.

"Let's go spy on the other side," Lana said Dwightlike. She
knew this would keep him indoors a bit longer.

They headed over to the acrobats and saw an array of critical
clusters at various removes under the marble twins.

"They are looking kind of chesty," came the honeycomb
drone of Rene Vukovitch, thick with knowing. "It's because the
corps girls are all on the Pill."

"He's always declaiming like that," Dwight informed Lana,
"so everyone will know how inside he is."

Fernanda Levine was with Rene, tossing her hair that
was too long for her age (around forty), shifting her plump
weight from leg to leg with a sway that looked stylized. The
one time Lana had tried to talk to her, Fernanda looked
everywhere but at Lana. It was as if this array of personal
mannerisms—shifting weight, tossed hair, eyes looking away—
kept her unrooted, near the door. Yet she and Rene were
always together, one of those intense intimacies between a
solitary woman and a gay man. No eye contact problems
there.

Dwight and Lana switched their attention to the larger circle, a padded cell where Cassandra Rogers was cushioned by
her trio of Cassettes, two females midforties (competing for
teacher's pet, shining the apple with their sleeves, so to speak),
and a younger man playing the prince, ready to kiss the hem of
her gabardine skirt. It was fascinating, their body language, a
ballet in itself. They were hovering, maneuvering, running an
intellectual egg-in-a-spoon race, neck and neck. They were

plotting, stalling, longing for that tragic day when Rogers retired and chiseled the name of her successor—*my* name, each hoped—in stone. Is this what it took to win? Is this what you had to do?

"It won't be one of us," Dwight said, reading Lana's mind. She nearly spurted her sip of seltzer.

"How did you know I was thinking that?"

"I'm Cajun, I'm gay, my god is Tennessee Williams. Of course I knew what you were thinking."

"Ready for your cigarette?"

———

Dwight insisted on smoking two cigarettes. "You're from Chicago," he said to Lana's shivering on the outdoor balcony. "A New York January should be kid stuff to you."

They both had to scurry to their seats as the lights dimmed, but being on the aisle meant you could be late, plop down. That was one of the beauties. The other was the unobstructed view. Also, the thrill. Fernanda pretended not to notice Lana's little flounce of lateness, to which Lana thought, Ignore me all you want. She was enjoying her first night on the aisle. In fact, she was having more fun with Dwight at intermission than she was watching the stage. Seriously, she had to concentrate. She had to start taking better notes with her new red pen. She'd written only one thing during the first ballet—"where's the fire?"—'cause the dancers didn't look *in* the music, they looked like they were running away from it. But that wasn't An Idea. Anyway, this next was what the critics were here to see, a corps girl's debut in the company's Cliffs Notes version of *Swan Lake*. The lights came down.

Going out the second time was slower, because of the clapping and curtain calls for the debut. When Lana finally found Dwight, he was already heading for the balcony.

"There's someone I want to talk to" and she followed his glance to a cute blond in tight jeans standing outside. The "cute boy" was a gay-world ideal pronounced as one word, cuteboy—a species that flourished at the ballet. Nothing came between a queen and his cuteboy, even if the cuteboy didn't know the queen existed. Lana bowed to the obsession, but not without whining: "You're making me stay in here *alone*."

"Think of it as a reconnaissance mission," he said, nodding toward the acrobats—"bring back dirt."

Lana went and got a cappuccino so she'd have something to do with her hands, then wove her way toward the cliques, standing near enough to observe, but far enough away to feel invisible. It was pretty much the same scene as before, only this time Rene had joined the circle around Rogers. But where was Fernanda? Not anywhere that Lana could see. No, there she was, making her way through some clumps of couples (East Side couples, given the shine on the women, big gold earrings, big gold buttons, salon hair, and nails lacquered like reflectors). She could see that Fernanda was hearing Rene's voice. They could all hear his voice.

"That music is not from another score," he snapped, his wave of impatience aimed at the younger man. "It's usually cut, but was spliced back in." As Rogers's princeling had just been cut and spliced.

Fernanda was making her way to the voice when she saw it

came from the golden huddle. She stopped in her tracks about five feet away. It could have been a mile. There was no way that locket of shoulders would open up for her.

It was known that Fernanda had tried with Cassandra and failed. They were too much alike. Willful brides of ballet. Cassandra was the original, and Fernanda, original too, refused to be a copy. And so the rift began. And widened when Fernanda sent Cassandra copies of *Divertissements* and Cassandra sent the packet back unopened. At which point Fernanda published a parody of the song "My Favorite Things"—by "Rodgers and Rogers"—which began

"Darci in *Diamonds,* and Peter retiring,
  Misha in *Murder* and Pina expiring . . ."

and had the whole dance world hooting, not just Dwight.

The strange part was Rene: he alone could go between the two women. He'd been in Rogers's circle when Rogers was coming up (in the days when he himself was a cuteboy) and yet he never became a Cassette. And while he was totally close to Fernanda now, intermissions saw him rounding into Rogers orbit, on some magnetic curve or mystic undertow.

What would Fernanda do? She stood there, saw herself stranded, then slowly began to turn away, only to meet Lana's eyes watching her. It was a long second and Lana winced out a smile. Fernanda swayed, a form of hesitation, then took the few steps over.

"Are you liking the dancing?" she asked Lana. It was one of those general questions that are complicated to answer. Lana ducked it.

"To be honest, I'm having trouble concentrating. I haven't settled into the season yet."

"I know what you mean," Fernanda said, though probably she didn't. Fernanda might be fidgety standing, but in her seat she was completely calm and focused.

"And you?" Lana asked, trying not to sound as if she needed to know, just curious.

"Jenny's Feet"—Jenny was the debut—"the feet of life and death."

This is what Rene and Fernanda did, Dwight had told her. They would take possession of some piece of anatomy, they would see the eternal flame in some gesture, and they would make a fetish of it. It was their own little world of totems and taboos. And very effective too—it made you feel all the more outside for not having given whatever it was its full meaning and importance.

"You mean that gorgeous arch?" Lana asked. "It seems to spring out of her ankle, not below it like most people's do." Lana had noticed how the girl's arch had a swan's-breast sweep and fullness. "Like her heart is in her arch."

"It's so Odette."

Dwight was right when he said "they always have to have the last word, even if it's a throwaway." Still, Lana was feeling for Fernanda. Here she was, if only for the minutes Rene said his hellos and dropped his latest gossip, waiting like a wallflower. There were chinks in the Royal We. It was as if Lana was seeing Fernanda for the first time. She had beautiful green eyes.

"Hello," Rene said, returning with not an atom of interest in Lana. Fernanda swiveled madly.

"Rene, you know Lana Burton, don't you? We were just talk-ing about Jenny's feet." Fernanda then turned to Lana. "What did you say? Like her heart is in her arch?"

"Yes-it-is-a-beautiful-foot," Rene replied in one note, having none of it, though Lana bet if she wasn't there he'd be waxing rapturous over Jenny's Feet.

"I'm gonna head back," Lana said—well, she had to say something upon leaving.

Lana went looking for Dwight, who was maybe still smoking on the balcony. If he was with Blondie, she'd leave him be. She pushed out into the cold.

"There you are." He was alone with his cigarette. "What happened with the blond?"

"He went for something prettier. What happened inside?"

Lana, hugging herself for warmth, described the whole thing in detail, Fernanda's sticky situation, her snap decision to come over and make nice.

"Interesting . . . ," he said, taking a deep last puff, and then blowing smoke upward into the black sky. "But watch it."

Lana was listening.

"She may be more vulnerable than Cass, but they both play for keeps. Don't get me wrong, I'd write for Fernanda. She's the outsider. It would be fun."

"Then what's to be afraid of?"

"They're both ego monsters. Agree with 'em—fine. Cross 'em—not fine. Cass'll just look right though you, and with Fernanda, you'll be one of those big falling-outs she's always having."

"But look at Rene."

"Right. Look. And learn. He's close to Fernanda, he has

history with Cass. So what does he do? He keeps one in check with the other and takes what he needs from both. He's a walking, talking survival instinct. You let yourself get taken up by just one"—Dwight flicked his dead cigarette into the dark—"and you have to take up their fights. Which gives them all the power. And then they dump you the minute you disappoint them."

"I know," Lana said as they went in. "Beware agendas. But how do you know when an opinion is also an agenda? Who's the judge?"

"You are, my dear. And it's a slippery slope. So don't end up on your butt."

And Dwight would know. He was a mountain goat in the slippery slopes, always his own man.

"See ya at the Saturday mat," he said, striding off.

Into her seat for the last time, Lana was surprised, but not entirely, by the warmth that greeted her return. This must be the flip side of Fernanda.

"I saw your recent piece on musicals," Fernanda said.

"But no one saw that piece," Lana said, incredulous. "You had to fly somewhere to read it."

"People send me clips. I like what you said about dream ballets. I love anything with colored toe shoes."

Lana nodded. In classical dance, toe shoes were pale pink, pure, but on Broadway they ran the gamut—red, yellow, green, black, blue.

"Theater people respect ballet but don't trust it," Lana said, "so they put it in a pretty box, all tied up in colored ribbons!"

"Ballet in a box," Fernanda agreed. "You know, *D* always needs new writers." She flipped to a blank page in her notepad, then held it out to Lana. "I'll call you."

Lana wrote down her name and number with her new red pen.

The Perfect Day

One never quite recovers from a happy childhood. That's what Iris had been thinking lately. She would never say this out loud, of course. These days there was so much awareness of awful upbringings. And the memoirs that were now all the rage, hair-raising tales in which women (they tended to be women) described a frightful coming-of-age. For so many people, there was little in the past to gaze back on with pleasure, to warm their hands against; exquisite little to enjoy unwrapping and rewrapping in white tissue, as Iris had done with her Christmas things, now that the holidays were over. Iris wasn't exactly sure what she meant when she thought you didn't recover from a happy childhood—and God knows she wasn't complaining, only trying to put her finger on something. It was that goodness could haunt you too. Boundless early love could leave you vulnerable later on, expecting, assuming, that everyone loves that way. You had to keep learning they didn't. And those brimming years—birthday presents and Easter dresses and endless Indian summer in northern Illinois—as they receded, they seemed to be leaving you heavily behind.

Her childhood had been full of horses and hay and fox hunts and pheasants and good dogs and bad dogs and molasses. Iris had learned lore from alcoholic grooms who fell off the wagon every half year or so, but in the months in between taught her how to remove a rusty nail from the bed of a hoof (you had to squirt in turpentine as the nail withdrew), how to "bean" a horse (you reached up the gelding's sheath, all the way to the elbow, and gently worked out the little lump of matter that had gathered over the year), how to French-braid a tail (the tricky part was starting). She witnessed absolute power in the person of the stable owner, a lean yet deep-bosomed Barbara Stanwyck type who loved money, hated fear, and bugged her barns with a hoary old intercom system so that she knew what the kids were up to. Tucked in her heated office above the barn, with her frost white hair and beady, ice blue eyes, she was God in Her Heaven, invisibly monitoring the activity below. The kids, plotting insurrection in whispers, never felt safer. To this day, when Iris happened to crack open the old tack box that was taking up too much room in her coat closet, that world of pure security would be back in a breath, and that dust peculiar to stables—a moist, gritty mix of hoof dirt and horse dander, ancient cobwebs and atomized manure—like pollen from paradise, would crowd her nose and make her sneeze.

As a girl Iris was allergic to nothing. She had been a bold and industrious child, setting herself all kinds of projects and, unusual for a child, finishing them. Iris remembered long afternoons with her sisters, making outfits for their Barbie, Francie, Scooter, and Skipper dolls (they weren't allowed to have a Ken doll because he was "too mature," just as they weren't allowed to see Elvis Presley or James Bond movies). They'd make the dolls walk, talk, stand, and sleep, because you couldn't do much else with those scissor-straight legs. In Iris's doctor phase there was the refurbishing of stuffed animals (sewing seams, patching holes) which she treated like major surgery, complete with a pre- and post-op gravity that kept her younger sisters silent with respect. There were even the neighborhood bumblebee hunts Iris would organize, each child equipped with a mason jar. Iris now couldn't remember why she was driven to catch bumblebees, except perhaps in revenge: she once got stung on the toe.

Iris's parents never figured in these events. In her memories they remained disembodied voices in the background, eternally indoors or down the hall, a timbre of safety, a shadow of protection. They came into focus at mealtime, on family outings, helping with homework, and quite close-up in the car. There, thought Iris, was a picture of mid-twentieth-century childhood: the his-and-her silhouettes of two heads banked against gray leather, Mom and Dad chatting in the front seat. Strange what an image of equilibrium it was.

They never knew of Iris's favorite project, one she did alone. She called it The Perfect Day. This was something larger than the intricate play typical in a household of all girls (their brother wasn't born 'til Iris was fourteen), and Iris only tried it once, twice, a year at most. A Perfect Day would be keyed to a special event—like the first spring horse show—or maybe to a constellation of events: the October Saturday that began in the morning with the hunt club's Blessing of the Hounds and then ended that night with the high school home-coming game. In the weeks leading up to a Perfect Day, Iris would make a list of everything there was to do in her life: clean her room and her drawers, finish all homework, polish her tack and buy new hoof picks, weed out her wardrobe and plot a way to get that new sweater to wear to the football game with her girlfriends (never a date, Iris wasn't allowed to date until she was sixteen, not that anyone was asking). Nothing particularly overwhelming here, but all together, an undertaking. The idea was to have everything in her life done—no chores or disorder—so that she could enjoy the big day without a wisp of worry or regret. In a way, these days were her first creations.

Did she achieve perfection? Not really. Chance got in the way—a book report assigned the day before, a stain on her favorite breeches that hadn't quite come out, a bad schooling on her horse Britomart. It didn't matter. Iris sighed at the magic of those days, the clean, feverish approach to what was always a Saturday, always daytime and cloudless, and always beaming with possibility.

She remembered her wedding to Erich this way. How handsome he'd been at thirty. How his wrinkled khakis hung on hipbones thin and sharp as seashells. How he walked across the U. Penn campus almost with a bunny hop, an upward jerk with each step that made his stride excited, should have made him look silly but instead was strangely sexy and made you want to skip alongside him, to catch the ash from the cigarette dangling from his mouth, the ash that glowed and dropped like his latest brainstorm in the lab. His colleagues were awed by his elegance in experiment, unnerved by his cold stare, his even colder logic. Oh, Erich wore his rue with a difference. "Voodoo science" was his label of disdain for peers who couldn't repeat their findings, who didn't keep up their lab books, who schmoozed. He was a dervish in the lab, dancing smooth amid his gels and silver stains. He once came home with a radioactive thumb and was careful not to touch Iris with it, for two weeks switching sides in bed so he could hang that thumb over the edge and still be on his back. He became that thumb. Hanging over a void, and Iris at arm's length.

The Perfect Day. Iris had the society pages to prove it. Their wedding on a bright and cool October afternoon, light the color of Lillet. Erich in his grandfather's morning suit—a perfect imperfect fit. And she in a Callot Soeurs she'd picked up at Christie's, ankle-length ivory satin with breathtaking trapunto work, a wreath of orange blossom on her head and in back a whale spray of tulle. They looked out of Fitzgerald, everyone had said so. At the reception an old Biddle aunt took Iris aside to describe Erich in the days when he rode, the rakish way he sat a horse. Iris still had Erich's oxblood field boots in her trunk, the ones he'd thrown into the garbage to make a pointless point, which she'd retrieved in the night. The legs were long, teenage tubes, the mahogany leather worn honey-colored on the inside of the calves. When she put the boots on they came way up over her knees. Like a musketeer.

Iris had kept only one photo from their wedding album, the one that showed them emerging from church and had been published in both *Town & Country* and *The Philadelphia Inquirer.* She loved it for the way he was holding her hand. His big hand clasped over hers. She could still feel it, too tight, but Erich always did everything too much, and in that moment, their hands a knuckleball in the air between them, she felt his happiness.

Erich had stopped riding and hunting in college for the same reason he stopped doing a lot of things. It was no longer logical: he'd experienced it; repetition didn't intensify a feeling, only diluted it—on to the next. Iris didn't like this mode of thought, and didn't dwell on it, sensing that eventually she'd be the bore he needed to move on from. Anyway, animals were now for cutting up. She'd never forget the day she surprised her new husband at the lab on a Saturday, with a picnic lunch and a thermos of cider nipped with brandy. This was what young wives did, didn't they? And the Penn campus in autumn was achingly beautiful, especially the old Medical School, all that old stone chiseled into trefoils, gargoyles, and Gothic arches that put you in your place. The intellect was eternity, the stone seemed to say, the individual, dust.

She'd walked into the lab (odor of stale sulfur; test tubes cloudy with use) feeling like Faculty Wife Barbie with her twinset, ballet flats, and wicker basket looped over a pale fore-arm. The labs were empty except for one assistant who pointed to the far end of the hall, the room where the rats were kept. There was Erich, actually wearing a lab coat (which he never did, deeming it novice) and with a big brown horse-hair-looking mitt on his right hand. He gave her a nod, not even saying hello, as he picked up a thrashing rat in that mitt, stepped over to a gleaming aluminum contraption sitting on the counter, stuck the rat's head in a steel hole the size of a quarter, and decisively, in an almost buttery motion, brought down a foot-long lever with his left hand. A sickening crunch was the last thing Iris heard before she hit the floor.

"The rats aren't happy about this either," he said as Iris came to with a brine blast to the brain—smelling salts. Erich explained that he had thirty rats to kill, thirty brains to slice onto slides and freeze, and the more he killed the more hysterical the rats became, because they smelled blood (she noticed a Jackson Pollock splatter on the arm of Erich's lab coat). Therefore he had to move fast—no time for a picnic. There never would be time.

Iris took her picnic alone on the campus lawn, turned her face to the warmish breeze but lost heart at the chicken legs, the image of her head bent over a bone. She wanted to be with her husband, to laugh with him—not gnaw away by herself. It was the first on a continuum of solo Saturday afternoons in Philadelphia—squintingly sunny or rainy gray, sky blue or snow white, all heavy with that span of time from one to five, an arc of isolation. Iris got used to the upbeat leave-taking, the "march on, darling" stoicism of the workaholic's wife. She got used to telling herself he couldn't stop an experiment in the middle just because his wife was waiting. She never got used to those Saturday afternoons.

But the mail sailed in—society fund-raisers, sorority news-letters, university reports—to Mr. and Mrs. Erich Biddle or sometimes Dr. and Mrs. After all, he was a PhD. If only he'd been a real doctor, like her father. Iris never voiced this thought. She felt like a traitor just thinking it. But a medical practice was grounding, stabilizing. You had to deal with people. There was something precarious about benchwork, something too much in sync with Erich's abstract, erratic side. Pure science rewarded risk, the trip to intellectual Antarctica. When she leafed through Erich's lab book, she met a flow of numbers coursing in long columns, a momentum mapped with arcs and arrows, all written in his torrential hand pressed hard into the page. It was difficult to believe that any single blood cell, any scrap of tissue, was the trigger for this outpouring of signs and symbols. Encoded in these columns were measures of receptors—muscarinic, dopamine—those sites of anxiety and elation, sadness and joy. The secrets of human emotion were here, inside these numbers. Erich was here.

And then the overwhelming load of grants with their huge monies that had to be managed, appropriated, divvied up among the careers of postdocs and lab assistants and MD-PhDs playing with science became, in his words, a drag. Students begged to work with him, only to grow bitter with the concentration he demanded in the lab, with his inability to stroke and flatter. He didn't get it, couldn't coddle. He drank too much at lab parties—always had actually—but now he left slurring. And still he was in the lab by eight every morning. He published paper after paper in *Science*, in *Nature*, yet avoided the head of his own department, a fiftyish sultan of science, knee-deep in yes-men and their sly wives, a glittering-eyed pasha who would have loved a Biddle under the expansive arm of his Savile Row suit. Erich was silent at staff meetings, sullen, but increasingly a key speaker at symposia in Sweden, Tokyo, London, LA. At thirty-five he was at the top of his field, feted, respected. At home too, respect. And a remove that confused and frightened Iris.

To this day she couldn't say what happened, where the twist or omission in Erich had occurred. Did something happen in childhood? Did his own dazzle exhaust him early? Did he simply, chemically, not care? He had been a tender, attentive lover early on, smoking slowly in the dark; over time he was still tender, but his mental preoccupations, plus the habitual last drinks, plunged him faster into his trench of sleep. There were no more nighttime murmurings, no more sharing of dippy jokes and dreams. If only she could have slipped a bit of his own brain onto a slide, what would he have made of that math? And what about her? Could another woman have reached him, steadied him? Another woman not so insulated by her happy childhood, her belief that people always come through?

And then his lightning lab work was shadowed by schemes that Iris could only call hare-brained—Ralph Kramden–ish get-rich-quick schemes, weird patents in the works, unlikely and fleeting alliances with agriculture, the military. Except that Erich already had money, his trust. The long slow quest of the test tube, well, the enterprise had lost its glow. Erich went off to a World Health Organization seminar in Tanzania and found a new grail, another glow. He gave his talk to a crowded room and when the lights came up he didn't even hear the first question, he didn't say anything, just removed his tie, draped it neatly over the podium, unbuttoned his collar, and walked out. For days after no one knew where he was, what he was doing,

and Iris's long-distance calls to Room 608, increasingly anxious, went unanswered, her messages swirling, or so she imagined, in a front desk cubbyhole like a small square blizzard,
spilling out onto the floor like a public display from which you
looked away, and the operator's voice maddeningly flat with
every mounting call until Iris was told oh yes, there was a message left this morning: "Checked out, no forwarding address."
And then everyone knew. He was chucking it all for an emerald mine—raiding his trust for a deed and two John Deeres. It
was a shock, a joke, a loss, and a disgrace. It made sense to no
one but Iris, who had to admire, however absurd, the clean
and bloodless cut. After seven years of marriage, seven years in
which she watched everything come to nothing, she was now
Deborah Kerr in *King Solomon's Mines*.

There was nothing else to do but return to New York, the
only city where people might pay for Iris's level of lamp shade.
She rode in with the movers, which was nice of them—a
thirty-four-year-old woman seated between two young guys,
high above the road. She told them about her first move to
Manhattan, right after college, how she drove a little U-Haul
from Illinois, and how terrified she was by the turnpike traffic
pushing her from behind. She was having fun making them
laugh. But in the sweaty spiral into the Lincoln Tunnel,
bumper to bumper, Iris was quiet. The sun was so hot. And
when they emerged from the tunnel's bathroom cool the sun
hit again like a slap. It was Saturday, honking and dirty and
swerving, and Iris was back.

Designer Shoes on 2

Lana and Fernanda were shopping, an undertaking always a little tense for two women over thirty, be they sisters or friends. To shop pleasurably together required true camaraderie, an easy intuition when it came to subjects like weight and wallet. This would not be like shopping with Megan, where certain things had become running jokes, like Lana's endless fretting over shoe size, her left foot vaguely, maddeningly, larger than her right ($8\frac{1}{2}$A or B? Or 9A?); Megan's habit of buying clothes a tad too small since she was always about to drop that last five pounds (but never quite did). They knew each other's flaws and knew when to say nothing and when they could laugh. Megan knew Lana had an impossible waist, which no matter how much exercise she did or weight she lost was twenty-eight inches and had always been twenty-eight inches and would always be twenty-eight inches. Lana knew Megan had a little extra padding above and to the rear of each hip and Megan called these her "shelves" ("I could serve tea on these things"—a vast exaggeration). Lana's waist, Megan's shelves, Lana's straight hair ("lanky"), Megan's Irish waves ("kinky")—these were enduring landmarks in the country of their friendship. And then there were the gifts from God, like their both having nice slim ankles, a gift no money on earth can buy. But with Fernanda, the physical inequities were greater, the financial question . . . well Lana didn't know what Fernanda made, only that she didn't make much more than Lana and couldn't count on any help from her parents, even in an emergency, which was a huge disproportion. Lana would have to be very careful shopping with Fernanda.

Their friendship had begun at the ballet—that January night when Lana had talked to Fernanda during Rene's ten-minute defection. Three days later Fernanda called Lana and asked if she would write a review for *Divertissements*. Lana fell over herself on the phone, saying of course she'd be thrilled to be in Fernanda's pages and it was an honor and no, the twenty-five-dollar fee was not a problem, she'd write for *D* for free, what was the assignment? Nothing earth-shattering it turned out. There was a new *Dance in America* broadcast coming up, so how about a piece about dance on television? Not the kind of subject on which to peg a tour de force. It didn't matter. She'd be in the pages of *Divertissements*. She was, on some level, accepted.

Lana turned it into a short essay comparing old studio stills to moving images on videotape. She wrote about the sculptural properties of black-and-white photographs, how the dancers seemed carved from mist and shadow—lush illusions—while dance on TV was like a Saturday morning cartoon (the Hanna-Barbera *Magilla Gorilla* kind), flat and lacking in effect. Fernanda said the essay was "deeply piquant."

"What do you think that means?" Lana asked Sam. "Deeply piquant."

"It means it's stylish, maybe more stylish than she expected. You should take it as a compliment."

But more complimentary was the way Fernanda was calling Lana to talk about performances. Well, first it was performances, then work (Fernanda, like Lana, held down a tedious editorial day job), then it was the male dancers Fernanda had crushes on, then the father, the mother, the brother, Cassandra, the past. In mere weeks—here it was March—they were confidantes.

Lana was a little cowed by Fernanda, there was no question about that. She knew Fernanda could argue circles around her: she was a PhD from Berkeley who'd written a dissertation on *Piers Plowman* (Lana had never heard of it and imagined some rustic with an ox). Fernanda left all that behind when she flew to New York for a job interview and discovered the New York City Ballet instead. She traded the ivory tower of the university for the enchanted forests of ballet, and like a needle to a groove applied her academic habits, her gift for the carrel, to the subjective and voluptuous world of dance. Combine this doctoral doggedness with a deep need for attention and you had a terrifying drive. What could Lana, with her BA from a good Midwestern college and her direct, dispassionate view of the stage, possibly offer Fernanda?

Exactly that, her direct, dispassionate view of . . . everything. Many daily phone calls into the friendship Lana realized that what she gave Fernanda had little to do with dance. It was Lana's steadiness that attracted her. And also the pretty embroidery of her upper-middle-class upbringing, her trips to Saks and her teas at the Stanhope. Fernanda, deep within her infrastructure of defense, her thick dark hair a kind of cloud cover against darts of humiliation and doom, sensed Lana's carefulness with others—and her pride in that carefulness. The very thought that Lana could shield Fernanda from Cassandra and the Cassettes, from her childhood and herself, gave Lana a new understanding of her status as Sensible. Fernanda, the academic never at a loss for a line, was a shaky-legged lamb in the rest of her life. Lana was the shepherdess, watching for wolves.

And so they were at Bergdorf's looking at shoes. The second-floor salon was a place Lana had always loved. With its slipper chairs and sofas modernes, all upholstered in a rich beige, it was like a module in a luxury spaceship, still much the same as when she'd come to New York with her parents in the late seventies (just Lana—Tom and Livia were in college), and watched her mother try on beautiful butter-suede shoes with no thought to price, wanting new shoes for dinner at La Grenouille, a reservation Lana's father had made two months earlier.

"My mother at my age never had to consider the cost," Lana said as she examined a pair of turquoise Manolo Blahniks, on sale at $275 and still a stretch. It could be such a jolt—turning a shoe over to see the sticker on the sole. You braced yourself, pleasantly surprised by anything under $250. Lana cast a glance at Fernanda, to make sure her comment about her mother hadn't seemed like bragging. But Fernanda was fine, intent upon the same shoe in pink.

"What color would you say this is?" Lana asked, handing her the pump. "Not quite turquoise."

"Oh I'd say Bluebird. Very *franco-russe*, very Petipa."

"Yes. That's exactly it. A kind of French blue—like opaline. Have you ever seen opaline?"

"Tell me," Fernanda ordered in her need-for-new-data voice, "what opaline is."

"It's this kind of glass they made in France. The antique shop near my apartment has some. It only comes in blue, green, white, and I think a dull pink. And it has this shine. The white is sort of like a hard-boiled egg that's peeled, but is still underdone."

Sort of like you, Lana thought, looking into Fernanda's heart-shaped face.

"The thing is, you don't see colors like this anywhere else."

"The medium is the message," Fernanda snapped happily. "I need to see some opaline. Where can we find it?"

"They might have some on the seventh floor. In the antiques section. We can go there next. You really like pink, don't you? Is that because of toe shoes?"

"I do love pink," she said slowly, and Lana could feel her go inscrutable with pleasure. Fernanda courted notice, longed for notice, but she was not actually comfortable with notice once she got it. Lana knew all about Fernanda's father. Like the bill after dinner, their late-night phone conversations inevitably led to him. He had been Compulsively Seductive, Fernanda told Lana, had Crossed Boundaries (verbally, not physically). As a child she was always trying to win the unwinnable. In other words, she learned how to win on his terms, how to be equally seductive and charming, and how to drop out with no warning. For Fernanda, all relationships since had been a dangerous kind of leaning out over a ledge. Fall or pull back?

She fell once in her twenties, into the stale embrace of a much older English professor, his off-campus flat full of overflowing ashtrays and orchids postbloom, terminally stuck in that stem-and-dirt phase. Certainly he was erudite, and Lana imagined they had spirited conversation before they walked single file into the bedroom where he breathed cigarette breath into heavy wet kisses and finished in five minutes. (Since Fernanda wouldn't discuss whether or not he was good in bed, Lana assumed he wasn't.) But he did get her pregnant. And when Fernanda called to tell him (Lana imagined this act of courage coming from a campus pay phone) he sighed into the line cold and martyred and said it had to end anyway, he'd pay for the "procedure"—that cowardly euphemism, that lifeless word, from a man who wrote reams on "the moral mind" in Shakespeare. Twenty-seven at the time and still living at home, Fernanda never fell again. When she left California it was as if she left her body behind with the surf and the sky, and brought only her brain to New York. As for her heart, her passions were lavished on unavailable beauty: ballet's young

Apollos (she adored them from the aisle), and the married men in her Adult Children of Alcoholics program—a program Fernanda had no reason to be in technically speaking (her parents never touched alcohol), but went to all the same, feeling at home in this private community of pain.

Fernanda had a wide little foot with an exquisite high arch of which she was quite proud. On more than one occasion she'd slipped off her shoe to point her toe for Lana, to show off that arch, a curve any dancer might envy. It was the only part of Fernanda's plump and heavy-bosomed body that was dancerly, and it was the only part on which she splurged. She had black suede Arches, Yves Saint Laurent T-straps, and a pair of Delman green satin flats with rhinestone bows. She was eyeing the pale pink Blahniks with love.

"They'd go with your pale pink suit," Lana said, offering a nudge in case it was needed. "You could try them on just for the fun of it. And if you have to have them," Lana brought her voice down to a knowing whisper, "you could open a charge account and get that ten percent first-day discount. Which would make them . . ."

"Two hundred forty-eight dollars."

"Yeah. The thing is, though, pink suede is a magnet for dirt, so they're not for everyday."

"And this heel is high for me."

"Now that you say it, I've never seen you in a heel that was higher than three inches. If that."

"Well two and a half to three inches is the perfect proportion for me. Higher and the ankle line distorts."

Lana beckoned for the pink pump, then surveyed the heel.

"It looks like almost four inches. But the fact is, everybody gets Blahniks cut down. I read that in the *Times*."

"Hmmm. Let's keep looking and then I'll decide if I'm going to try them on."

Fernanda may have had less money than Lana, but when she made a financial decision, she never looked back. Lana was a little dubious about the pink, however. That suit wasn't really a good color for Fernanda. Her ivory skin, green eyes, and black hair salting up needed stronger hues—cobalt blues and malachite greens, fuchsias. Fernanda's ancestry was Russian Jewish. She should be swathed in the jewel tones of *Scheherazade*. But Fernanda's preference was pastels, wafty and weightless, pink and peach and celery-stick green for the celery-stick physique of a dancer.

They moved slowly around the rim of the salon, stopping in front of each shelf, appraising the flats, the pumps, the wedgies, the Ferragamos and Chanels.

"Shoes are like lipsticks," Fernanda said, "no matter what is happening in between, your feet and your mouth can always be beautiful."

"I remember the first lipstick I ever wore," Lana jumped in. "In high school. I thought it was the most gorgeous color in the world. It was kind of peach and frosted. It must have been awful. But you know, I thought it would change my life."

"And did it?"

"Of course not. I was just the same old me with frosted lipstick. But what I really remember is the possibility living in that tube."

"It's funny that you use the word 'living,' " mused Fernanda, picking up a little black pump with a Sabrina heel. "I've always loved the way lipstick swivels up out of that dark tube and leaves its mark on your mouth."

"A kiss," Lana said.

"Or a stain. There's original sin in lipstick—the snake climbing up the tree, and the mouth outlined on the apple."

"*That's so true!* The snake is a spiral too."

"That's why lip gloss is such a bore," Fernanda said, "gooey stuff in a little plastic . . . pit. You stick your finger in it." She shuddered flamboyantly, fanning out her small white fingers in disgust.

"So do you remember your first lipstick?" Lana prompted. They had plunked down onto a sofa at the far end of the salon, near the five-hundred-dollar golf shoes that no one was looking at. Fernanda, comfy in the well-feathered cushion, crossed her legs to show off one of her dainty ankles.

"My first lipstick was given to me by my Aunt Sada, my father's sister. She stopped by our house after having been shopping in the city. I was thirteen. She'd been to I. Magnin and bought a lot, and she gave me this little kit of Elizabeth Arden samples. You know my mother never took me shopping. Never once."

"*Whaaaaat?*" asked Lana in mock amazement, rocking a little on the couch. But there was no mock about it. Fernanda wasn't playing for effect.

"My mother didn't drive and never left the house."

Lana fixed her eyes on Fernanda and sat up a bit straighter, to show she was listening.

"I don't think she ever wanted to be married and she certainly didn't know what to do with me and my brother. She lived a sliver of a life. She was a phantom in a housedress. My father was her go-between with the world. I never saw her buy anything."

"Fernanda, that is really . . . unusual."

"So when Sada brought in those packages it made an impression. A woman out in the world, spending money on herself. And that freebie, it was nothing to her, but to me it was so beautiful and special. I remember my mother watching us with this look of disdain. Like we were dupes for thinking any of this mattered. Lipstick, perfume, blush. She just sighed—one of her waste-of-time sighs. And all she had was time."

Lana had once seen a picture of this mother: sitting at a kitchen table, arms bare, unsunned, fleshy white like something under a log. Unloving—but loved by little Fernanda, a dark spark of fire. Never Taking Her Daughter Out! It was grotesque.

"Fernanda, I don't know what to say, except how sorry I am for that girl."

Often after revelations like this Fernanda's green eyes would pond with tears, her voice would wobble. But not today. She sat matter-of-fact, cushioned from the memory by the luxury around her, the golden upholstery and the walls of beautiful new shoes, Cinderella singles awaiting their mates. She smoothed her hair. Lana decided to go upbeat.

"Do you remember the colors?"

"Oh yes. There were two. One was coral, called Sunfish, and one was sort of white—I thought I'd died and gone to heaven. Dewdrop."

"White! They should have called it Dracula. Fernanda, did you wear the white?"

"Well, everyone did," she said.

"And did you have the white go-go boots?" Lana continued, verging into a riff that would have amused Megan.

Fernanda watched her.

"And I bet you knew all the words to 'These Boots Were Made for Walking.' "

Fernanda performed one of her sudden swivels and said, "I think I'll take another look at those pink shoes."

She pulled herself up out of the cushion and left Lana leaning warmly toward what was now an indentation in the seat.

Lana trailed after Fernanda, over to the other side of the salon. "I love the fact that you remember the names of those lipsticks," she said to Fernanda's back. "Maybe Dewdrop was a premonition." Dewdrop was an important role in *The Nutcracker*, a dazzling debut role.

Fernanda had the pink shoe in hand and was looking at it hard.

"I have to think about what you were saying to me," she said to the shoe.

Lana felt a sick sort of uh-oh. She knew something had happened on the sofa. Maybe she should have asked a follow-up question about Fernanda's mother, not changed the subject right away. It was always a tough call—when to leave a painful subject. If you moved on too soon, you trivialized it. Lana stood there, waiting to hear what Fernanda would say next.

"It seems like you were making fun of me—all that stuff about the white lipstick."

"But that wasn't making fun."

Fernanda now looked at Lana.

"I don't understand why you would laugh at me after I told you about my mother. When I never discuss her with anyone."

It was like getting a big red F. Instead of protecting Fernanda, she'd done the opposite—she'd hurt her. And yet Lana knew it wasn't totally fair. Yes she'd made the decision to be playful, but the shoe salon at Bergdorf's was not the place for shock therapy. Fernanda waited, still holding that wrong-for-her pink pump.

"Fernanda," Lana said softly, stepping toward her, "you know I understood the import of what you told me. And if I shifted tones too soon, I'm sorry. But about the lipstick, I was just teasing you."

They were both quiet. Fernanda returned the shoe to its glass shelf, and Lana decided how to play the silence.

"Fernanda," she announced, "I don't think you know how to be teased. It's a form of affection, you know, but you do have to learn it. My parents insisted that we all learn to take teasing. Is it possible I'm right?" And then Lana knew she was right, and in an exaggeratedly teasing tone, said, *"You are not used to being teased."*

Fernanda had to smile.

"The thing is," Lana continued, "it can go too far, and then it becomes a weapon like anything else, but I really don't think I went too far."

"Noooo," Fernanda admitted, light coming back into her voice, her heart back in her heart-shaped face. "You never go too far."

Lana heard those words with renewed pride, and also a catch on the word "never"—a little thorn. She knew it was inevitable she would let Fernanda down. She knew it was in Fernanda, like a dye, to be let down.

"Let's go see the opaline."

CHAPTER TEN

Horse Story

Iris had on gray leggings, a gray fleece jacket zipped to the chin, and a blue knit cap. Her running shoes, recently replaced, were still absurdly white, like toothpaste. It was March—a winter, so far, of no snow.

Running wasn't allowed in Gramercy Park between nine and five, which suited Iris fine. She liked to run at the end of the day—six, seven, sometimes even eight—to get the kinks out. Today being Sunday, she was dressed and ready at 4:54. I'm just running to run, Iris thought as she crossed Twentieth to the park. Turning the lock with a big silver key, Iris pushed the wrought-iron gate open, slipped in and around, and pushed it shut. The heavy clang when it closed was like something in Sing Sing.

You had to consciously close that gate—hear the lock

catch—which could be difficult to do when someone who didn't have a key, who didn't know it was a private park for which you paid dues, who just wanted to sit in a charming spot for ten minutes, began to go in after you and you had to motion "no." It never felt right. Iris had learned to explain, "you need a key to get out too"—a kind of apology. People who snuck in were trapped inside. You'd hear them yelling across Twenty-first to the doorman at the Gramercy Park Hotel, or see them peering hopefully through the crusted window of the empty caretaker's shed until they finally gave up and approached strangers in the park. Iris had let many people— thankful, anxious, angry—out through that heavy gate. It didn't matter that New York was a city of privileges bestowed or withheld, which New Yorkers knew only too well and mostly accepted. Some things you couldn't accept. Like Iris's friend who'd actually started crying at Dean & DeLuca. It was the holidays, and as this woman—a respected art book editor who made zip—watched young wives piling up meats and cheeses and cakes and caviars in their baskets, racking up bills of hundreds just for food, and there she stood gripping a paltry bunch of baby carrots—her big purchase—tears stung and she left. Pretty little Gramercy Park had a similar effect. People felt that iron gate around green grass—felt it keenly. When someone was near the gate, Iris kept walking until she reached the next gate (there were four) and let herself in there.

Iris had a membership at a nearby gym, too expensive but convenient and clean. She used the gym for cardiovascular and free weights, a fifty-minute regime Iris loathed but forced herself to do twice a week because it was better than getting slouchy posture or flabby arms (your arms go, but they don't have to go fast). The treadmill, however, was just too boring. In any weather, Iris preferred to run in Gramercy Park. She liked the feeling of running in fresh air. She liked pretending she was a horse in fine form.

It was a silly thing to do, but it made her feel a girl again. It brought back those make-believe days before she had her own horse, when she and her sisters would turn the far section of the backyard into a show ring, setting up jumps made of cardboard boxes, lawn chairs with broomsticks laid across them, anything, and then have a horse show. They trotted, they cantered, they jumped. Their upper half was them—hands holding imaginary reins—their lower half was the horse. Like a centaur. If you changed your horse, you tried to change your cantering style at least a little. It was great fun, especially when the jumps got high. When Iris was given a real horse, Britomart, she knew she could stop playing horses, but she didn't right away. They were two different things.

Running for exercise in Gramercy Park, as her stamina increased, it all came back. The thrill of strength, the fun of covering ground, your mind roaming. Iris would begin her run thinking of nothing but where she was—the city path with plantings on both sides, the season surrounding her—but often the day would grab hold, the technical problems she'd had with a lamp shade riding along. As the rhythm of running took over, without actually thinking of it, a solution would materialize in her mind, another construction to try the next morning. It was amazing. Other days, she'd find herself mentally preparing for a difficult phone call, defending herself against the complaint of a testy decorator. These conversations always began with Iris sharp and sarcastic, which gave her seconds of satisfaction. But with every circling of the park, the edge was rubbed away and her responses became tactful, rational, calm. By then, her anxiety was softened.

Just about every run ended with Iris as Britomart pushing toward the finish. "Come on, Britty," Iris would say under her breath when she felt herself flagging. "Keep going." And days that were particularly beautiful and she felt particularly strong, she longed to up the ante, to jump something, or at least break into a canter. But then people would think she'd hurt her leg; or maybe they would know she was playing horses. (Would they? she wondered.) So she kept trotting, which was the same as jogging, and contented herself by lifting her chin—Britomart champing at the bit. On days when she had no energy it was lots of "come on, Britty, come on." And here she was forty.

It was her own pastoral, her own horse story. And Iris had once had a shelf full, read and reread. Where were those books now? *Black Beauty. Come on Seabiscuit. Copper's Chance.* Always about a horse or a girl fighting against odds and winning. There were two great horse-story illustrators from her childhood. Paul Brown, who drew in ink—he had a high-strung, slashing style—and C. W. Anderson, who seemed to use a soft lead pencil mixed with sunlight, a melting touch that made you want to kiss those silken muzzles, embrace those noble necks. Iris loved Anderson's drawings, loved the way each horse had its own character (Brown's all looked alike, they all had flaring nostrils). She especially loved an Anderson book called *Afraid to Ride*, about a girl who takes a nasty fall and gives up horses. "A bad horse took it away; a good horse will give it back." This line, spoken by the book's handsome Mr. Jeffers, she'd never forgotten.

Well it was so obvious now, what these horse stories were all about, and what the bad horse was a stand-in for. Iris couldn't think of Erich as bad, though. She wouldn't have married a bad man.

"Oh Iris, you're so stoical," her friends would say as if it were an irritating habit. "Maybe you should talk to someone." Always "someone."

Iris knew full well what they were driving at. They thought "stoical" was just another word for "denial." But what if it was? Iris didn't want to go round and round in a whirlpool of recrimination. Iris didn't discuss Mark either, the first man she thought she—well, she had—cared for after her divorce. Now there was a bad horse. A documentary filmmaker in a scratchy Harris tweed, he'd come to Iris's apartment to tape her for a PBS show on New York decorators, the Sister Parish segment (Iris appeared for all of ten seconds). He teased Iris, calling her "my bluestocking, blue-collar girl," because he thought covering lamp shades a curious sort of sweatshop work. Iris curled catlike to this winking warmth, amused by his teasing. Which amused him in return. It was very cozy, his eyes, pale hazel, locked on hers, intensely hazel (almost green), eyes people had admired her whole life. She felt seen. And you could go ages in this city unseen. Yes, he was less serious than Erich, but maybe, Iris thought, she should give Less Serious a try. Everyone was always telling her to. And the ways he and Erich were alike—quick, articulate, and Easternseaboard lean—put Iris in sympathy with him. Anyway, he gave her the rush and her head was turned. She just assumed he understood the kind of woman she was and what she needed. After all, they weren't teenagers. She was thirty-six, he thirty-seven.

And then he wasn't so nice. "So clue me in," he said one Sunday brunch, lifting a martini. "How does one start Monday morning in a sweatshop?" And he wasn't generous either, always taking her to cocktail parties and promotional gatherings that cost him nothing. And every date feeling like the first, ever so slightly rattled, as if he might not like her when he showed, which was usually late. It never got comfortable. And yet Iris gave him the benefit of the doubt, sorry for him that he felt the need to be snide, worried he felt small because he couldn't spend more.

Deena, suspicious from the start, blurted, "Are ya sure what team he plays on?" Which offended Iris, for Mark and for herself. Why would a gay man in New York in the 1990s go to the trouble of dating women? But Deena had seen what Iris couldn't, that Mark was a Very Available Man. Four months in, when Iris called his apartment and a young man answered, she realized just how available. It sank her. Scared her. She'd been so ridiculously trusting.

Even thinking about it now, years later, Iris flinched at her stupidity. But she did learn her lesson. She wasn't going to do what so many women did, drift from one iffy man to another. To friends who wanted her out and about, sampling the smorgasbord, the more the merrier, she shook her head no. You could have wonderful chemistry with a man, then learn he was a cad. You could have everything in common, and no spark. In Manhattan with its millions, people could live double, triple lives. You never knew. Iris began telling herself, a little mantra that somehow made her feel not so alone, if it's meant to be, he will find me.

"Come on, Britty," she said, running faster, pushing to finish her last five minutes at a clip. Sprinting at the end was hard, but it wiped the mind clean of everything.

Now you can stop, Iris said to herself, having sprinted the last four laps. She kept walking, to cool down, then took a park bench near the shed, not ready to go in. The light was staying later. It was the end of a gray Sunday, not warm, not cold, the type of almost spring day that tempts you to ride your horse outdoors, even though the ground hasn't thawed and will be too hard on the horse's legs. Iris remembered how cooped up she and her friends would be feeling, stuck for months in the indoor arena, cantering in circles; how that first glassiness in the air lured them out into the forest preserve where they ended up pulling their horses off the path because it was still frozen, a stiff grid of tractor ruts, some filled with old snow that crunched like Styrofoam; and how their horses—not happy being turned into a forest of poking, naked branches— jerked the reins and kept backing into the stumbling path. Oh that strange sensation, that helpless drop into space when a big horse backs up in blind rebellion. Iris leaned her head back against the bench and stared into the high bare branches of Gramercy Park, such a cold canopy of limbs—stripped, exquisite, deaf to everything. Except, it seemed, the twilight.

"Sudek," she said.

Iris had bought a huge book of Josef Sudek photographs last September—the Poet of Prague, he was called—bought it in a kind of trance. The book was almost one hundred dollars, but she had to have it after she flipped it open and landed on a page of winter trees in snow, the black branches spun fine, almost microscopic, like inky optic nerves in clouds. She felt herself sinking into the image, a catch in her breast that was almost sexual, the desire to be joined with this world. And then she glanced at the date and was shocked that it was 1955, not the turn of the century as she expected, but just three years before she was born. This heartened her. There will always be my kind in the world, Iris thought, few as they may be, susceptible to the spirit in things. There were no humans in Sudek's late work; the pictures were peopled with glass eyes and mute eggs, mist on windows and empty benches. And branches.

Iris reached her hand up, superimposing her spread fingers on the full moon lurking behind one tree.

I could make a lamp shade of branches.

If a transparent bulb were underneath, it would throw gangly, ghostly shadows around the room. But it can't look craft shop, like a souvenir from Wisconsin. It has to be distant, mysterious, with capillaries and gaps, the way it looks now. I can try. If anyone can do it—Iris dug for the key in her pocket—I can.

Honey West

Lana was in the library. She was doing research for an article on *Le Martyre de Saint Sébastien*, a Debussy and D'Annunzio extravaganza from 1911. It was a pagan miracle play with music, about the saint who was tied to a stake and shot full of arrows. It was also a famous theatrical disaster, five hours long. "Yikes," Lana thought, "those poor Parisians." Luckily, the concert version of *Le Martyre* was just under an hour. Then again, reading D'Annunzio's libretto flat on the page was its own form of torture.

"Remember the star that was nailed to the living heart of heaven."

Arrows dipped in absinthe, fin-de-siècle swoons, writing soaked in blood and wine. Not to Lana's taste. She was feeling a kind of library anxiety, unchanged from childhood—that wanting to leave and knowing you can't because you have more reading to do, more wandering in the stacks, more photocopying. And what was it about the overhead light in libraries? It hit you like a draught of laudanum. The New York Philharmonic had requested Lana for this article. Bathed in pure flattery she accepted, even though she knew it was a short deadline, due in a week so they'd have it for the June program, six weeks away. Lana had told herself it would be a good stretch. Too bad she didn't feel like stretching. It was a crisp, spring Saturday and she felt like shopping for a new tote bag.

"Aim well. I am the target."

I can't read another word, Lana decided, eyeing the new periodical computers sitting unused on the far side of the room. They were twice as big as the library's computers for books, and they had huge blue screens, not little gray ones. Lana scooped up her pile of books so no one would cart them off, and crossed the room with an air of purpose. Let's see what everybody's up to. She settled in, glanced around to make sure no one she knew was in the room, clicked on "author," and typed in the name "Moore, Sylvie."

Lana hadn't spoken to Sylvie since that Friday tea last October, exactly six months ago, when Sylvie, well, what is it Sylvie actually did that day? Blew up? Threw in the towel? *Le Martyre de Sylvie!*

Lana had thought a lot about that tea. She'd analyzed it with Sam, and then on the phone with Megan, and at the time it seemed as though she and Sylvie had just hit the limits of the friendship. Or maybe "relationship" was the better word. Because in a way they weren't even friends so much as two

clever women feeling extra clever together. Lana knew nothing, she realized, about Sylvie's situation vis-à-vis children. Or
anything else in life that really mattered. She didn't know,
actually, what Sylvie wanted from her work. She knew what
Max wanted: Sylvie in the glossies. And what about Max?
Whenever Sylvie spoke of him her tone turned jokey-sexual,
like they were such a hot couple. Why did she need that? Over
time Lana began to feel she never understood Sylvie, that
there was a weakness, a masochism even, that made Sylvie
push you into a place where you would push back. Like this
was a game Sylvie was used to playing, a game she didn't mind
losing. Was it the usual thing, a person who enjoys being the
injured party? Lana liked to think herself a student of character, pretty quick, but with Sylvie she'd been oblivious. What
was it Lana had said? Something like, "They don't use my kind
of writing." There was leeway in that line and Sylvie turned it,
like a knife, on herself.

"I am the target!"

Oh Sylvie, Lana thought loudly, you wouldn't in a million
years want to do this tedious piece on D'Annunzio—my kind
of writing. Even I don't want to do it.

Whatever the psychodrama was that day, Sylvie never called
back, and Lana, having left three messages, had to take the
hint. Or rather, the hook! People in New York always said, "No
answer is an answer, too"—it was a big-city cliché. Still, Lana
did miss Sylvie. She was funny, with a quirky mind. And
though difficult, she was easier than Fernanda, whose self-
worth hung in every balance, and whose emotional need, at
first so tentative, had in the four months since they met taken

wing as fully fledged Rights of Friendship. Fernanda required an almost liturgical support, often ending a narration of her day's run-ins and face-offs with the question "Am I a bad person to feel this way?" and Lana always answering (*Law and Order* rerun on mute), "You're not a bad person."

Furthermore, where Lana and Sylvie could talk about men from a similar perspective (they both had one), Fernanda pretended Sam didn't exist. On the one occasion Lana tried to get the two talking—dinner out before a concert—Fernanda refused to look Sam in the eye, not difficult to do when you are performing the Hair-Tossing Ballet. Sam, chewing dutifully, looked mostly at Lana, while she sat anxious and stymied, a chess pawn between two kings.

The computer was slow, searching, its tiny hourglass pulsing, then it blanched blue-gray and a list popped through the void: Sylvie's junk journalism over the last year and a half.

Hmmm. There were her first glossy pieces, including the *New York* magazine piece that got *Vogue* interested. And then three *Vogue* pieces right in a row, beginning with Sylvie's cerebral profile of Judy Davis. Lana had read it; it was good. A story on Sandra Bullock—sort of forced, but then, could anyone make a strong case for Sandra Bullock? And then a piece on Jenna Elfman. Lana hadn't seen that one (and was glad she hadn't—talk about a ditz). And that was it for *Vogue.*

Now this was odd. Here were two recent articles that had nothing to do with actresses.

"Scents and Sensibility," *House & Garden* magazine. It was described as "a literary garden—perfumes, scented rooms, and fragrant flowers in the stories of scandalous French writer

Colette." Lana remembered that Sylvie had taken a class in French wines. But when did she become an expert on Colette?

"Tea and Sympathy," *Glamour.* "Why don't women take men to tea? The author suggests men are the perfect tea-mates, sexy and sympathetic." Well that takes the cake! Maybe Lana was being narcissistic, but she did feel this was a jab at her.

It was surprising that Lana and Sylvie hadn't crossed paths in all this time, assuming Sylvie was still going to the theater. Not that Lana wanted to cross paths. When it came to such confrontations she was hopeless. She always felt the same sensation: as if her face were swelling up and the air around her body was solidifying, locking her into a stilted, self-conscious posture. Lana knew she was nonconfrontational. She could be tough in the office, but that was part of the job: she was fighting for her writers (and sometimes *with* them, like when she assigned fifteen hundred words and they turned in three thousand). As a critic—on the page—she could confront to her heart's content. But in person, honestly, she didn't get off on getting her way, though it sometimes seemed everybody else did. Lana liked the feeling of being unseen, of slipping through crowds like water. As a girl, Lana's favorite book was *Harriet the Spy.* Harriet, with her round glasses on her round face making her daily rounds with a spy diary everyone resented. Lana had loved Harriet's freedom to move around the city, her freedom to see what she saw. So Lana began skulking around too, keeping a notebook of blunt observations, though suburbs are not so good for skulking. Instead of fire escapes and corner stores, it was endless open lawn, bushes in front of windows, and basically nothing much happening. Plus everyone knows who you are.

And then there was *Honey West*, a TV show starring Anne Francis as a blond spy. Lana knew of it before she ever saw it, because Livia had watched the show first time around and referred to it as the be all and end all of style. "Honey's an adult Harriet," Livia said. "She only wears black and has a black panther she walks on a leash." (When Lana read that Ida Rubenstein, the Jewish heiress who starred in *Le Martyre de Saint Sébastien*, had kept a pet panther, all she could think was, "like Honey West!" Which was, of course, backward.) Anyway, when the show returned in rerun, Lana was transfixed by Honey and made her mother buy her a black velour top which she wore with black tights. She'd sneak around the house in this outfit, pretending she was on missions, hiding behind doors and under desks for what seemed like hours, but were probably minutes, finally getting in trouble when she witnessed Tom singing "Pinball Wizard" in front of a mirror so that he threw a book at her and broke a lamp. Lana was grounded for a week—"for invading your brother's privacy." Even now, her mother sometimes called her Honey West, as a reminder.

From there it was *The Avengers* and *The Man from U.N.C.L.E.* Lana and her best friend, Sue, pretended they were Napoleon Solo and Illya Kuryakin, communicating with secret signs and code words. When Sue's younger sister wanted to join in and they said no, she said, "Then I'm Emma Peel." Lana and Sue were speechless. That brat—the superb Emma Peel?! But there was nothing they could do. The brat had beaten them to the punch. It was a law of childhood: if you claimed the character first, it was yours. So they claimed April

Dancer, *The Girl from U.N.C.L.E.* Still, because they took her by default, she never seemed as cool as Emma Peel. When Sylvie compared Lana to Diana Rigg at the party where they first met—she had no idea the tingle.

At one time Lana talked about really becoming a spy, working for the CIA. It was then that her father suggested she read *The Spy Who Came In from the Cold.* It was just the three of them at table—Mom, Dad, and Lana (Tom and Livia were off at college)—those days when Lana was the lonely voice of youth speaking up to a father who was too used to being the robed voice of wisdom, and the milk-glass light over the kitchen table shining too white on his need to guide his youngest child.

"Panthers aside, Lana, a spy's life is lonely and dangerous. You think it's glamorous, but it's not. Mata Hari never looked like Greta Garbo and she ended in disgrace. The French firing squad." Which had still sounded pretty glamorous to Lana.

She loved her father, and he was attentive to her, but that was just it. His time with her had the feel of quotes around it, not the easy way he was with Tom and Livia, not the way he beamed over Tom, rolled his eyes over Livia's histrionics. Admittedly, he was an introverted man who relied heavily on Lana's mother as a kind of aide-de-camp. Maybe it was that the twins, being twins, made more noise, generated more movement, created more camouflage for him. Whereas Lana, toddling into the room, or later, home alone—well, she was one concentrated kid, and had a way of bringing quiet into the room with her. "Where did you come from, Lana?" he often asked when she was little and had been off by herself for a while. He asked it out of curiosity, gently, or amused. But it really was, if you thought about it, an odd question. Especially seeing that, in some respects, she was more like him than the older kids were. In fact, on that first date with Sam, at the point when they were kissing those wonderful kisses at her door, all she could think over and over again was, Sam Kellogg, where did you come from?

Lana squinted at the screen, thrown by the shift in Sylvie's subjects. She exited, then called up some of the Cassettes (who weren't up to much it turned out). She finished with "Burton, Lana," and almost laughed at her list. One piece— Glinka. Lana knew this didn't reflect her true output. Her pieces weren't listed because they were in smaller journals, or publications like the airline magazine that didn't make a national index. Still, it was a little deflating to see only one article. She looked back at the clock. It was twelve-fifteen and she was hungry.

After running out for a quick yogurt and banana (she almost got a hot dog), Lana returned to her martyrdom, nibbling at shortbread biscuits she had stashed in her pockets, telling herself she'd work until three o'clock, then go to Bergdorf's, a twenty-minute walk from the Lincoln Center Library. She was getting a handle on the material, could see where she would go with it. "Whoever wounds me most deeply," Sébastien says in Act Four, "loves me most."

According to musicologists, Debussy's *Le Martyre* was in some debt, musical and poetic, to Wagner's *Parsifal*. Both works existed in a trembling dimension of Christian-pagan mysticism. And both contained wounded heroes. This was what Lana would focus on, how the "sacred wound" was a metaphor for the revelations of religion, the callings of art. It was Debussy's letters that got Lana going in this direction. In one of them, a discussion of piano playing, Debussy said the fingers must "penetrate the notes." Lana loved that, it was so abstract and yet so physical. Fingers *in* the notes, like sound in the ears, arrows in the body, and transcendence in the soul. She had to be careful. There was a sexual dimension to all of this, and the people at the Philharmonic were notoriously conservative. But why write, Lana thought, if I'm just going to think and see what's already been thought and seen. Lana knew—the way she knew so many things without knowing why—that this was the right path through the piece. And anyway, it was Debussy who'd given her the key. That's why she loved writing about the arts—there was always a key.

At exactly three Lana was up and out, just like school days. It was a clear day, nippy for April, and she set a brisk pace down Broadway, crossed at Columbus Circle, and walked along the Central Park side of Fifty-ninth Street, which had the superficial cheer of bad cafe paintings: colorful, half-seen tourists; carriage horses with feed bags and red plumes; spring branches tremulous overhead.

At Bergdorf's Lana didn't stay long in handbags. When she was newly arrived in New York, she used to buy here all the time. Not anymore. It hurt to admit it, but she could no longer afford this store except for sales. Luxury goods had skyrocketed, while Lana's yearly raises barely covered cost-of-living increases. That was the arts, that was journalism, that was reality (unless you got a contract at *Vogue*). Lana looked in the glass showcases, asked to see two totes in particular, the plainest two, and neither was under five hundred dollars. She'd have to go to Bloomies or Saks. Anyway she had too many other expenses coming up, Sam's birthday for starters. There was the new Alan Ayckbourn play he wanted to see. She could probably get freebies for that. But there'd be taking him to dinner after (that would be a hundred). Plus a present.

Part of Lana wanted to get home—Fifth Avenue stores were so frantic on Saturdays, everyone wired in a weird hurry, this feeling of Time Running Out—but another part said: you're here, cross the street to Bergdorf Men's and look for something for Sam. Maybe something cashmere. A hat. Sam never seemed to have a hat.

The men's store was a relief, the space and calm letting you set your own rhythm. Lana drifted among the glass cases, from one containing expensive alligator and ostrich wallets to another filled with enamel cuff links, striped and dotted like tiny jockey silks. She compared some cashmere scarfs—a gray windowpane plaid, a camel check—thinking the gray was a possibility at $275. Except a scarf in spring was a little late. A blue knit cap was nice, but alone in a box it would look skimpy. She'd check out shirts and sweaters. She took a step down the stairs then stopped. A few yards off, facing away, was the unmistakable beacon height of Sylvie, white hair striking above her black mohair wolf coat. Lana reversed fast and slipped backward around the corner, feeling like there were searchlights on her.

This was too typical of New York. You think how you haven't seen someone in ages and the next minute you run into them, as if you'd conjured them up. Lana stood stiff, then inched around. Sylvie was still facing away and seemed to be examining a folded shirt on the counter, then turned right for a moment. She looked the same, her brow and hands as pale as ever, but her hair was longer, not a white wing anymore, now swept back into a drifty kind of French twist. She was the only one in shirts—except for a tall man who had just come into view, just right of Sylvie. Great, thought Lana, until she leaves I can't look for a shirt for Sam. Lana checked to see if salesmen were noticing her skulking, but no one was. Maybe if I wait a bit . . .

Lana peeked again and this time she noticed that the backs of Sylvie and the tall man were side by side at the counter, as if they were looking at the same shirt. Sylvie tipped back her head, laughing. Then in statuesque slow motion she turned her face to him, showing that marble profile, and smiling that silver curve of smile.

They were together.

He wasn't Max.

A salesman appeared and the man gave a quick nod, held up two fingers, then pulled a wallet from under his fitted coat and handed over a card. While the purchase was being rung, the man turned to Sylvie and very softly smoothed a stray tendril (left hand, no ring) up and back into her twist—like returning a baby bird to its nest. She looked at him as if nothing else mattered. Then the salesman returned with a big purple bag, and after a signature and a round of thanks, they left, not touching, by the side door to Fifty-eighth Street.

What had Lana seen? She waited a few more minutes and

then went down to the counter to scope out the shirt he'd bought two of. Three hundred ninety-five dollars. For cotton. This man was wealthy enough to drop eight hundred bucks on two cotton shirts, this man who wasn't Sylvie's husband, certainly wasn't her father, and didn't touch her like a friend.

Maybe the two had just come from tea—the Pierre at Sixtieth, the St. Regis at Fifty-fifth—and he was Parisian, hence the Colette article, the French twist. That overcoat he wore was a European cut. Maybe this was why no one seemed to know what Sylvie was up to these days. Or maybe Lana was way off and there was a harmless explanation. For instance, if this man *was* European, well, weren't those Romeos always smoothing tendrils, playing at love? Maybe he was one of her old photographer friends—they were always touching and fussing.

Still . . . the way Sylvie had looked at him.

When Lana saw Sam that night she would describe it all. They'd play amateur detective together. He'd say, joking, "Ms. West, why didn't you follow them for a few blocks?" and she'd say, "I know, I know. Why didn't I?"

But he'd know why she didn't. There was seeing and there was stealing. It was like a diary left on a table. You could wonder all you wanted about why it was out. You could pick it up and shake it and even push the button on the lock. But say it fell open! You were not allowed to go ahead and read. That was the code you learned as a kid. You had to close it and walk away.

CHAPTER TWELVE

Behemoth

Iris laid the folder down on the coffee table. It contained her taxes, just returned from the accountant. She looked again to be sure it was true, then closed the folder. It was the end of June (they'd filed for an extension) and she owed $2,800 more than she thought she would (new tax laws, no mortgage deductions, et cetera). Iris just sat there, stunned. Her health insurance had gone up, her rent was going up, and now this. Yes, she had the money in savings, but that was for other things, a new evening dress, a vacation, an emergency (but not this kind). Iris had thought she was getting ahead. Now she was behind. She sat staring at the floor, then looked up. It faced her from across the room, impassive. Maybe now was the time to sell it.

She had found it in a furniture warehouse on Market Street,

not far from the U. Penn campus. It was wedged in among mud brown Empire-style dressers and 1950s bureaus with chipped veneers. It towered over the huddled reproductions around it, not only because it stood on its side (to save space) but because whatever it was (Iris had to tip her head sideways to get a view) it was authentic. The mahogany was ravishing, with the sweetheart sheen of taffeta. The pulls were glass, like abstract flowers, and they were all there, all fourteen. On each end of this thing there was a mahogany column, elegant, Ionic—and under these, lion's paws with big fat toes. And what were those two vertical drawers, set in symmetrically on either side of three centered horizontals? Wine bins, Iris was told. Wine bins, she said to herself, Erich will be so pleased. The sideboard had just come off the truck and it was four hundred dollars.

"Why so low?" Iris had asked C.B., the huge, unhealthily soft man who worked in the warehouse (he looked like he was made of mushed Wonder Bread) and who had answers for everything.

"Because it's too big." The sideboard was seven feet long, forty-two inches high, and twenty-six inches deep. It *was* too big. Where did it come from?

"It's an old Philadelphia piece. Mahogany and cherry— solid. Must have been custom-made for a seven-foot space in one of those old town houses. Like the ones on Rittenhouse Square."

Iris didn't have to think. She pulled out two twenties—to hold the piece—and said she'd be back with the rest the next day. She knew just the place for it in their Society Hill parlor.

And hadn't she always said to Erich, when she'd meet him after work on spring evenings, busing the ten blocks up from her job at the auction house so they could walk home together from Penn—drifting through the campus breathing in the mimosa, crossing the silent Schuylkill River, cutting over from Walnut at Nineteenth to pass through Rittenhouse Square, all green velvet lawn and gray stone mansions—hadn't she always said, dreamy against his arm, "One day, when you're head of the department, we might live here." It required no answer. They both knew he was talking to Rockefeller U. in New York, Mill Hill in London, and Princeton was nosing around too. It was the "we" that was so lovely, a high perch with a long view from which he exhaled the smoke from his cigarette, easing away the day's still-clamoring calculations and computations. Or he might answer in kind, always the same, teasing: "We have to live somewhere."

Once the movers got the formidable thing into the house in Society Hill—got it up the front stairs, tilted just so to go through the front door, then hoisted high on end, momentously angled and pivoted between banisters and jambs, grunts and sweat, eking into the parlor where it was placed against the far wall—it looked as if it had been there forever. Everyone remarked on the sideboard, commenting on its size first, then its beauty.

"You could put a body in there!" said Zack Sarnoff, a microbiologist who was trying to write forensic mysteries on the side and could drink more beer than anyone in the lab. *Two bodies.*

"Erich calls it The Behemoth," Iris said, watching Erich

bring in a Coors for Zack and two Tanqueray martinis, up with olives. "I told him it was large, but Erich never made it to the warehouse to take a look. He said he trusted my judgment"— she gave her husband one of those fond-wife smiles—"but when he walked in and there it was . . ."

"Zack, put yourself in my place," Erich said, dropping into his leather club chair. "Would you have thought four hundred dollars could buy something so massive?! I was expecting, I don't know, an Old Philadelphia whatnot. I come home to Moby Dick."

"Man," said Zack, running his hand along the satin finish, "it's a lot o' wood."

Their friends just didn't know what to make of The Behemoth. The scale was daunting, baronial, stoically lonesome for old mirrors, pier tables, valences, tassels, rich heavy sauces and stiff maids in aprons. It unsettled friends who still had bongs stashed, well, stashed somewhere, who were only beginning to replace postdoc grunge with pieces from Crate & Barrel and Wanamakers. The Behemoth was a hunk of history, too substantial for where most of them were in their lives—in the lab pursuing invisible epiphanies. When they made their breakthroughs, proved their points, they might then want some history for their own homes. But now it was the future they were after.

"Look at it this way," Erich concluded, a philosopher's cock to his head, "if we're ever thrown into the street we can remove the drawers and live in the thing." To which Iris mouthed to Erich from across the room, "we have to live somewhere."

The fact was, Erich liked The Behemoth. He thought the

wine bins nifty. And the columns classical. And he liked it because Iris did, because she was so thrilled with her find and thought it so appropriate to the space they were in.

But bringing the thing to New York had been a trial. The divorce itself never saw court. Erich laid it all out for the lawyers in a letter from Tanzania. He gave everything to Iris it was in his power to give. Everything but two things: his club chair and the antique microscope that had brought them together (it consoled Iris that he would want it). The family was distraught and sympathetic, nevertheless they whittled down the settlement laid out in the letter and Iris—bystander in one of those endless, repetitive, near-to-waking, last-dream-of-the-night dreams—let them. She felt funny taking alimony when there weren't children yet. So the divorce went through in a daze, a flow of documents and decrees, Iris empty but sitting up straight as she signed, signed, and signed. Erich was absent all the way through. Except for the letter he sent her. It said, "Forgive me."

Iris knew when she married Erich that he was different. He was a lady killer who was completely faithful. (She loved that.) He was well read, had in college been torn between literature and science—like a nineteenth-century naturalist!—so they talked endlessly of poetry, art, with *The Notebooks of Leonardo da Vinci* ("The natural desire of good men is knowledge") their favorite. (She loved that too.) And his smile, dimples almost mythologically romantic—it was a smile with heat that made the world right. But the moods—what he called "brown studies" yet looked to her like trips to the interior, sunless descents. And the vagueness—what he called "thinking" and "making a living" and "science" and she called "not there" and "out of body." And the drinking, which she had taken for blowing-off-steam, a university habit he'd leave behind with marriage. This man she fitted to at night, bone temple pressed to temple, their arms like vines, and bottomless kisses that seemed to moat them in the dark—he could be within arm's reach at parties and yet she seemed to watch him from afar. When he returned to her from his deep retreats, that sculpted hand seeking the curve of her head behind her ear, there was something in the brightness of his eyes, a quickness like guilt, as if he knew one day he wouldn't make the return. And one day he didn't. He was finally, literally, off the map, and then the rooms in Society Hill were empty, all packed into a big truck, all except The Behemoth, which sat alone in the echoing space, the movers having left it for last.

The sideboard refused to come up the stairs of the Gramercy Park town house. It was a redbrick house built in 1860, and had a slim stairwell full of hairpin turns and an unexplainably low ceiling on the first landing. Iris had taken a tape measure to that landing, but she had never been good at geometry, and she didn't figure the added inches of tipping the sideboard to the diagonal, didn't foresee it stranded in that space the size of a phone booth. The movers brought it back down where it sat in the town house entry for five days, unnerving Iris, looking like a gigantic, fearsome folly.

This heap of wood stuck in the narrow entryway, an entry that belonged to others, it was just the last straw. It seemed to mock every certainty of the last seven years. Iris was powerless before it, shuddering with anxiety, and now helplessly indebted to her landlords (who were actually quite chipper about the situation). She was ashamed of herself. She was doing this wrong. She had done everything wrong. No wonder he couldn't love her enough enough enough.

On the fourth day, numb from not eating, surrounded by boxes she couldn't begin to unpack, as stuck upstairs as The Behemoth was down, she dialed the first name she found in the yellow pages. Two men arrived, respectively short and tall, quick and laconic, squirrelly and hazy, clearly fly-by-night but game for the job. They said the sides with the columns would have to come off. Iris knew she shouldn't entrust the sideboard to these questionable hands. But sick to death of it, she paid the two-hundred-dollar advance and as the men pulled out screwdrivers and mallets, she left them alone to manhandle the masterpiece. A day later, when it was back together in her new living room, The Behemoth had two bruises on its left side and a long crack. That was, of course, the side that showed.

With The Behemoth newly settled in the apartment's dining alcove, Iris fingered the bruises and felt remorse. The sideboard was majestic under her ten-foot ceilings. And Lord it held a lot. It was like a house—even bigger on the inside than it appeared on the outside. Just that spring, when Justin Howard, a new decorator on the scene and a new client, came over to firm up his first commission—an umbrella-shaped shade he wanted in butter-and-ivory stripes, *zig-zagging* (the kind of tour de force Iris was known for)—he headed straight for The Behemoth.

"*Where,*" he cried as if something had been stolen from under his nose, "did you find this?"

"In a warehouse in Philly. Around 1986."

"Whad'ya pay?" It was a dicey question between decorators, but as Iris wasn't a decorator he could ask and she could answer. Indeed, she knew the number would send him spinning.

"Oh Iris," he said, his tone heartbroken, "you could get ten grand for this today. With the market spilling out millionaires—the kids are dying for pieces like this. Big rich statements to match their big rich egos. Instant lineage. I have a young couple now, money coming out of their asses, with a four-thousand-square-foot loft, two hideous David Salles, and a shiny-shiny Art Deco bedroom set I finally talked them into selling, you know, after they gave me the old "just a few good pieces" line. Ten thousand dollars. They'd pay twenty for this sideboard."

"Even with the bruises?"

"That's character. You make something up. Tell 'em it's third-generation Biddle. They'll go blue." Whatever that meant.

"Justin, you're awful. Besides being unethical." But Iris already adored Justin, who shrugged airily, utterly unfazed. It was an affinity as old as the hills. Those with taste would always unite against those with just money.

It was odd though. When The Behemoth was stuck downstairs, she was ready to sell it for a sou. But in the years that followed, despite her endlessly tight finances, she wasn't the least bit tempted. And it wasn't because the jokes had stopped when she moved to Manhattan. Even here people found it intimidating. Like Mark. The Behemoth was not the kind of piece that made a cheap man comfortable. Those kingly paws, that rubbed-in burnish and mahogany blush—the sideboard suggested endless means, a magnate's pleasure in purchase. So instead Mark made fun, constantly referring to it as "the sarcophagus," which Iris was supposed to take as a tease.

Foolish was how he wanted her to feel. If she was in some way beyond his means, he wanted to make sure she felt beyond her own means too, holding on to something too large for the life she now led. He was trying to equalize things. And as women so often do in the beginning, she let him. She laughed and went along (and didn't discuss the years in Philadelphia).

But laughing at herself wasn't enough. It sometimes seemed as if Mark was competing with her, which Iris couldn't understand. And when he observed one day in the sunniest way, not a cloud in the sky, that it was "quite pretentious" of Iris to have kept the Biddle name, she was speechless. It was such a glib, belittling thing to say. He quickly retreated in "I'm just *kidding*" and "Who am I to judge what's in a name?" Yes, Iris thought, *who are you?* He'd relished going "behemoth" one better with a bigger word, "sarcophagus." He liked its implication of stone coffins and monuments to oneself. He was taunting, toying with, Erich. And he was nothing compared to Erich. The Behemoth was not only a piece of history, it was her history. She would not laugh at it. It was too big. It held too much. She had let it crack. How could she ever let it go?

Ultimatum

So Lana had done it. The morning after their second-anniversary date, a Sunday morning in May, she had sat Sam down. The six months had gone by, six months in which Lana was hoping Sam would rescue her from the moment by taking the initiative himself. In February, when they spent three days in Vermont at a country inn—long walks under skeleton trees, warm scones in front of embery fires, living together like married in one room—she kept thinking he might pop the question, *any question.* But he didn't. In April, when they took Amtrak down to Baltimore for an afternoon Orioles game—cheered, drank beer, ate burgers—then came right back cozily home, she thought maybe now, here on the train. But he didn't. The blockhead was perfectly content with the way things were, perfectly oblivious that Lana was waiting for anything (and, of course, unaware of the drama brewing, her dream ballet).

So when May came, Lana had faced the moment of truth so many times she was weary of it. That was why she prepped so hard. It was inevitable now. To fink out would not only be the worst personal cowardice, it might start affecting her responses to Sam. She didn't want to be a snipey female, pretending everything's fine when it isn't. She wasn't going to blame him for not giving her what she hadn't asked for. It was time to ask.

So she sat him down on the orange love seat. She'd worked it so he'd be over at her place, on her turf. They'd gone to see the revival of a Pinter play, then went for a late dinner at Film Center Cafe (a Sam Spade–type place Sam loved), and then walked up Ninth to her studio apartment at Fifty-fifth. She had cleaned like a fiend, bought a pretty new bedspread, pale green, and placed a big bunch of purple irises and yellow tulips on the table in front of the casement window. They weren't really noticeable at night, but in the morning, when Lana tiptoed over and inched open the curtains on the casement—only about a quarter of the way, to keep the room languorously shady—the light hit the flowers in a burst of joy that could be seen from bed.

When they were dressed and ready to go to brunch, that's when Lana sat him down. He had that look on his face that every man gets when a woman says "We need to talk about something." A condemned look that said what-have-I-done? and how-did-I-get-here? and is-there-an-escape-route? all at the same time. Lana proceeded as planned, not caring if she sounded corny, no games to protect her pride, no high horse, just a naked statement: "I love you. I want you. More than I've ever wanted anything. And I think it's time for us to go forward and live together."

He looked shocked.

She continued: "If you can't go forward with me, I need to know. Because I do want to live together, I do want all the things other women want, and if you can't give me this, I need to find someone who will."

"But no one," he blurted, "lives together in New York." This from a lawyer with a steel-trap mind.

Lana didn't roll her eyes as she wanted to. Instead she kept smiling and said, "Lots of people live together in New York."

"I don't think I'd be good at living with someone," he said. "I like living alone. And I'm not sure Spiffy"—his mean cat— "could deal with someone else."

"She does when I stay over," Lana said. These were school-boy excuses.

"I don't know about this."

He was shaking his head, but the funny thing was, he looked happy. There was no bad vibe in the air, no "no." There was only a feeling of expansion, like life had just gotten bigger around them, making them closer.

"You don't have to answer now," Lana said. "You can think about it. But don't make me wait too long."

And that was it. That was the big moment. They went out to brunch holding hands. They always held hands in the street, but that day when he took her hand it was like a pact—sealed by the May sun and the warm breeze. Over his eggs Benedict he narrowed his eyes at her, as if he were sizing her up, seeing her anew. Lana was just so thrilled to have gotten it out, to have done it, she felt all quavery and pleased, like she'd just run the marathon. It was one of the great moments of her life, no matter what Sam's answer, though deep down she felt she had already won.

They took a long walk in Central Park, the gray lanes closed to cars and full of Rollerbladers weaving, cyclists like human torpedoes, runners chugging way behind. They talked about this and that, but not about the ultimatum. They let that hang between them, untouched. And they ended the Sunday like any other, with Sam returning to his apartment and Lana returning to hers, both needing to get ready for Monday, parting with a hug and kiss at the cab, with Lana reaching for another last kiss.

Usually, though, it was Lana coming uptown from Sam's, the end of their weekend marked by the walk west along Twelfth Street, six blocks to the corner of Sixth Avenue, where Sam would put her in a cab. Lana had come to hate that walk—Dread Walk she called it, just to herself. It was always toward the end of the afternoon when the normal ennui of Sunday would drop suddenly deeper, like low blood sugar, because it was time for Lana to go home. They'd be back from brunch and from whatever else they did in the neighborhood, checking out new shops, shooting down and back from Chinatown, browsing in bookstores. Sam might be fiddling with one of his cameras, trying to thread film into his prized old Leica, cutting the film with scissors so it would catch into the spool (Lana would hear these mouse-scratchy sounds followed by

Sam's heavy sighs). She might be reading, flopped on his leather couch, or maybe just staring at his stucco ceiling, in which she sometimes saw shapes. But as the short hand neared four Lana could feel the moment approaching—"like an invisible spider," she told Megan.

Sometimes he'd look at her and say, "It's getting late . . ." or "I've got a big day tomorrow" (to which she wanted to say "Well, so do I"). Sometimes Lana would bite the bullet, would get up and say, "I guess it's time for me to get back" (to which Sam never said, oh stay a little longer, because to him they spent oodles of time together). They would head out and Lana would feel herself grow quieter as they got closer to the cab. It always felt like the end somehow—the way the walk west coincided with Sunday dusk, which intersected with "good-bye." It was irrational. A feeling of forever. Lana was confident of Sam, yet fought melancholy on this stretch of sidewalk. And the weird thing was, by the time she got home (it only took ten minutes rattling up Sixth), she was fine, happy to have the evening to herself. It really was the act of parting that upset her. And it was fear too, fear that the longer things went on as they were, the harder to jolt Sam into something more.

It didn't help that during the months leading up to May, the women in Lana's life, family and friends, had begun putting in their two cents, almost as if some emergency switch had clicked on. Lana had said nothing of her strategy to any of them, even Megan, because as usual she didn't want watching, waiting eyes. Or comment. Or advice. But not wanting these things didn't mean you didn't get them.

Livia: "You're thirty-five, kid. I know you think he's the

greatest guy in the world, but love is timing, and if he can't commit now, maybe he's not so great for you."

Mom: "Honey, don't wait too long. We want little Lanas running around. Little Honey Wests."

Deena: "Sam's takin' advantage, and it isn't like he's Matt Lauer or anything. If I were you I'd make him jealous. Start playin' the field. That'll get him back in the game."

Fernanda: "Is marriage something you want with Sam? I guess I didn't know that."

And Sylvie, Lana could only imagine what she'd say: "I can't believe Sam doesn't want to marry you. You're so great. Any man would want to marry you."

Megan: "The way he looks at you"—Megan met Sam on a visit to New York—"it's obvious he adores you. That doesn't mean you won't have to take control."

Megan's advice was best, as usual, because it was closest to the truth (Livia's was second, also true, but too heartrending to hold close). As for Deena and Fernanda, they weren't founts of wisdom when it came to men. Deena's advice was basically insulting, but that was Deena.

So after that Sunday in May Lana felt home free. All she had to do now was wait.

And wait. For after a month of Sam not making a peep on the subject, Lana realized she was back in the void. It sure didn't feel like win-win. And she sure didn't want to have to bring it up again. It was his turn. His job. Now she was peeved. But more than that she was starting to be confused. What was going on?

Lana tried to keep cool, keep her balance. She was working

hard at the office and on her writing. The quarterly she was doing dance for loved her first review, which was thrilling. Meanwhile, there had been a skirmish over her Saint Sébastien essay. The Philharmonic's PR lady, as feared, killed it ("I don't care what Debussy said, we're not printing *penetrate*"). With nothing to lose, Lana sent a copy of her essay to the young guest conductor who had programmed *Le Martyre*, an up-and-coming Brit. He thought the essay "rather ballsy" and insisted it be photocopied and slipped into each and every program. It was a rare triumph in the smoothed-and-sanitized world of New York classical music. It was also a little spotlight that put Lana on the map, especially when her essay was cited in the *Times* music review: "themes explored in a provocative think piece by Lana Burton . . ." Lana and Sam went to the last performance, Sam squeezing the knee of "my provocative girlfriend," and when they went to Cafe Luxembourg afterward for a celebration snack, Lana thought he might make it extra special by finally answering yes. But no. All they decided was to stay at her place that night, it was closer.

Lana had told herself that a month was pretty much what she expected to wait. But a month had passed three weeks ago. Now it was mid-July, hot, dead, heading for August—the dog days, her mother always called August. Something to do with polio, and staying out of the water.

No answer is an answer too.

Lana could no longer deny the possibility that Sam, as happy as he was that day in May, didn't have the stuff to go forward. She was coming closer and closer to that moment she had so practiced—like taking a vaccine—in the hope it would never be: "The simple dignity of her good-bye." She felt sad for Sam, how pathetic it was if they could be this close and still he wasn't ready. But for herself, well, she couldn't think it ended just yet: that would open an abyss inside. So she circled back to being confused by him and hopeful that there was still a chance. She was moment-to-moment dark then bright then dark, tears welling in odd places, like at Coliseum Books, where they first spoke, or walking by the old church near Lincoln Center, where they kissed during a downpour under the Gothic arch. To think of herself without him, not having him, breaking up in this sweaty Manhattan summer, the air-conditioning a droning comment on her loveless life . . .

The last few dates hadn't been easy, trying to be light and up and fun when her heart was heavy and down and defeated. Tonight at least they were staying in, so she wouldn't have to be charming in a restaurant. Sam was renting some movies and they were going to order Chinese. Lana stood listlessly in front of her closet, staring at her clothes. She was awfully shaky, teary. What was the point of these two years, to end like this? Why had she bothered to always look so cute? She checked herself in the mirror—despite everything she looked pretty, her brown eyes shiny and large, like a consumptive! *Très tragique*. It was a fact, most women would agree, those days you felt your lowest, you often looked your best. Why was that?

Usually Lana was quick to get to Sam's on Saturday night. Now, like a 45 record going at 33, her motion was slowed, her responses sort of grogged. She went into the bathroom, splashed cold water on her face. She took a deep breath in front of the bathroom mirror and squared herself—"You've got to be bright for your last night. You don't want him to remember you blubbering," which utterly crumpled her, made her really cry. More splashing, and then she put on a crisp white eyelet blouse over blue cotton capris, periwinkle blue, and some new white leather sandals Sam hadn't seen—they'd show off the slim ankles he was soon to lose.

There was a tinge of Last Time to everything that night. Lana usually took the subway down, but not wanting to arrive wilted in the heat, she took a cab, sitting not on the right side of the backseat but ceremoniously in the center. Standing at Sam's door, she listened to his usual last-minute vacuuming, that familiar white roar she always thought so darling. She let him finish, then rang the bell. They ordered their same order: chicken with pine nuts for Sam, moo goo gai pan for Lana. He'd rented *The Wild Bunch* and *Notorious*. Great choice, she thought, one about the end of an era, the other a romantic tear-jerker.

"Let's watch *The Wild Bunch*," Lana said. She'd have many long nights to weep over Ingrid Bergman and Cary Grant.

Sam noticed she wasn't her bubbly self.

"Are you okay?" he asked.

How stupid was he? But the timing wasn't right. She couldn't talk yet.

"I guess I'm tired," she said.

So he rubbed her feet for a good thirty minutes. And in bed that night, the room almost chill with the air conditioner set on high, he stroked her forehead, which always lulled her and led to long lush kisses, and then a slow cat's cradle under the sheet, his body a length of ardor locked in hers, and at the thought of losing him and this, a hot tear slid out the side of her eye and into her ear.

Sunday brunch—at the place they'd had their first date, the place they always went when she stayed over—was literally hard to swallow. All the heartbreak cliché descriptions are true, Lana thought, even as you get older.

It was really too hot to do anything ambitious, so they went back to Sam's after brunch. Anyway, there was a film noir he wanted to watch. The longest movie known to man, or so it seemed.

"It has the fedoras and the shadows," Lana said.

"But it never comes to a point," Sam said, completing her sentence. They always did that. "But we've watched this far, we might as well finish."

"*If* it finishes." But the longer it went on, the longer Lana had.

And then it was five o'clock and they were going down the elevator to the Dread Walk. They were out on the summer street. So here it was before her. Lana didn't even make it to the end of the block.

"I can't," she said, stopping, and of course her nose was instantly stuffed and her eyes filled. The tall town houses stood like silent witnesses. Sam looked concerned.

"What's wrong?" he asked.

She looked at his slate blue eyes that she loved so much and thought, how close can we be if you have to ask?

"I can't do this walk anymore . . . I hate it. I thought you were happy that morning when we talked, but you haven't mentioned it since." Tears tipped off her lower lashes. "If you don't want to move in together you have to say it," and then she paused to get control of her childish quivering chin, couldn't, and cried—*"so I can move on."*

And then she snuffled. The end of simple dignity. Lana couldn't remember feeling more exposed. But she couldn't stop looking at Sam through her tears and boy did he look sorry.

"I want to," he said fast, like trying to step in front of something moving, to stop it getting away. "We will." He was looking hard into her face, holding her eyes with his own, for reassurance. "We'll start right now. The paper's upstairs."

Then he turned her around and in the elevator back up he didn't say anything and she didn't either, she couldn't. He had his arm around her and kept squeezing her to his side—Sam's way of saying don't-cry, I'm-sorry, I-love-you. Tears were still going silently, Lana couldn't quite stop them. But now it was that strange, quiet calm you feel as a long-held fear recedes. He'd come through. They'd relive it later, not tonight but days or weeks later, hear Sam's side, why he'd waited, what he'd been thinking. This was him, slow off the dime, but there in the clutch. They hugged impetuously just before the elevator opened—then they walked the hall to his door. Lana thought maybe she could speak.

"September?" she wondered.

"September," he said.

The Tree

Iris was trimming her Christmas tree. It was a beauty this year—eight feet tall, graceful, with lots of air between the boughs. She was taken with it just as it was, naked in her living room. She loved the way the branches bristled in silhouette, gray-green needles combing the pale blue sky in the window. She was tempted to leave the tree naked, let it be the alien thing it was, a piece of forest from way up north. But two big boxes called from the closet shelf. Every year as the lids came off, Iris would see how well or badly she'd packed the year before. Last year, she'd been meticulous.

It was early evening. Iris had begged off dinner with friends. The tree was one of Iris's rituals and it couldn't be done in a rush. Before she could begin, the living room had to be neatened. Order, Iris believed, engenders order. She would put on music, usually *The Nutcracker*—it seemed to bless the occasion. Then she would pour a nice glass of red wine. Now, she could begin. First—the most tedious part of the job—the placement of the lights, a spiral from the top down. Next the garlands. Finally the ornaments.

Iris was always stunned by how uninspired most people's trees were. How many times had she been invited over for a Christmas tea or drink with the holiday perk: "And you can see our tree!" One assumed, then, that the tree was worth seeing. But Lord she'd seen some doozies! There was the shapeless, airless bush tree on which the ornaments were lodged, like stuff blown against a hedge. There was the suffocating fir, every square inch covered with ornaments old, new, borrowed, blue, plus doilylike things made, no doubt, in kindergarten (classroom art, the work of nephews sent by Iris's sisters, were plopped in boughs on the fireplace mantel, away from the tree). Iris remembered one number done by a neighbor, with red lights and tinsel only—an inflamed Cousin It. "How vivid," Iris had said a little too enthusiastically. Designer trees, well they were often the worst: Iris recalled The Year of the Magenta Bow, The Year of the Bronzed-Leaf Pinecone. "So clever," she would say to the proud owner.

Iris loved the moment when she lifted the lid on her own box of ornaments. She had never been a collector. As a kid she amassed two shelves of horse things—statuettes and cherished books—because that's what horse-crazy girls do, though she did notice that her friends' collections had a zeal hers lacked. She eventually learned she preferred the one perfect thing to rows and rows of similar things. But Iris did

collect Christmas tree ornaments. It began with her marriage
to Erich. Their parlor floor in Society Hill had such high ceilings that they needed a tall tree, and what would look more
chic on a ten-foot tree than those overscaled, organic shapes
made in the 1950s. They were out of vogue, so still cheap,
and they made thematic sense, since Erich was a scientist.
She'd scavenged Philadelphia for ornaments that looked as
if Kandinsky—or George Jetson—had designed them, ornaments shaped like parameciums and onions, as big as blown
brandy glasses. By their third Christmas the tree was a show-
stopper—like nobody else's—and the Biddle Christmas party
was an event in the department.

Days before the party Erich would watch the trimming sitting in his club chair with his string of scotches, would watch
Iris go up and down the ladder with her string of lights, listening as she recounted how special her father had made Christmas, how it was he, with his children as partners, who oversaw
the choosing of the tree, each of them taking a section of the
snow-crunchy, half-acre nursery, presenting their finalists,
then the committee decision to pick the best. Iris remembered
running through those arctic rows of tilting, steepled trees to
find her father and sisters in the maze, and then the debates
about height and shape and straightness as he pulled out tree
after tree with a gloved hand in the frozen sun, everyone's
breath icebox white. And then the decorating, which had its
own debates (do we want the star on top, or the spire?). On
Christmas morning, there would be four gifts for each child,
each one picked out by their father and mother together. Iris
could still remember them. That big book of fairy tales. Her

first saddle (oh, the smell of the leather). The love-knot sapphire earrings. And junior year of college, those wonderful Yves Saint Laurent ankle boots. Iris couldn't go into this too much or Erich might feel he was being compared to her father and not coming up to snuff—sitting there with his rocks glass, suggesting "a little left" or "higher," ice cubes clinking as he pointed. Well, Iris had never met any man as generous as her father. By their sixth year, Erich was reading while she worked, hardly looking up, sometimes nodding off. She tried to keep things interesting for him by making an exotic mulled wine, or serving caviar, or popping champagne, but for him this tree was old hat. She stopped telling her stories from atop the ladder. She stopped using the word "father."

When Iris left Philadelphia she took the ornaments, even though she guessed she wouldn't have twelve-foot ceilings in Manhattan. And anyway, she had begun collecting Victorian garlands, blown-glass spheres and pods, some striped like candy, threaded on waxed string. They were almost impossible to find, and getting expensive, but so sweet, so rich in character. Iris particularly prized those garlands in which the gold or silver leaf was dusting off like sugar, leaving an almost Venetian delicacy. In her first Decembers alone in New York, she'd spent whole Sunday afternoons restringing garlands, marveling at the thinness of the glass, a fragile state between frost and ice. She was amazed at the decades these glistering bubbles had weathered—in attics, in basements—and when she broke one accidentally she felt the quick crack of loss.

Regretfully, she'd leave her tree for a few days, spending Christmases back with family in Barrington, Illinois, where she'd arrive in that lonely limbo, the insider who's also an outsider. Every year, as she stepped through O'Hare's sliding doors into the Chicago wind chill, the slapping cold reminded her she'd been gone (in New York City you forgot what freezing really was). Every year, as the car headed northwest on the Kennedy Expressway (Mom used to pick her up but now hired a limo service), the office buildings constructed during Iris's teens, big new buildings then, seemed to have gotten smaller, as if the huge Midwestern sky was sitting on them, squashing them. Entering the house by the back door where the steps were sinking, a house too big now that all five kids were out and their mother never remarried, it always felt odd, off. And before Iris could set her bag down, her mother would be at the fridge, eager to warm up leftovers, new casseroles out of *Good Housekeeping*, when all Iris really wanted was a cup of hot coffee and time to see what was the same and what had changed.

Usually there was less than the year before. Bored with material things and wired for the present tense, Mom had retooled the holiday to something looser, less expectant and more convenient. She didn't put the green and red bulbs in the outside lights anymore, a signature tradition when their father was alive. She had to be coaxed to the Christmas Eve service at eleven P.M. (yet was always glad when they got there). And the artificial Christmas tree that appeared in the foyer—that was simply a stab to the sensibility, exacerbated when Iris saw her mother was decorating it with papier-mâché apples from the local tchotchke shop. "Oh Iris, *please* let it rest," her mother had complained. "It's too much trouble carting that old box up from the basement. And I think the apples are charming."

The tone of the household didn't come right until the first sibling came over with spouse or child or dog. Then Iris was absorbed into the noise, the endless plans of who would drive here or there, who wanted coffee from Dunkin' Donuts, what was the schedule for Christmas Day, and let's take the kids bowling the day after, et cetera. At this point Iris (Auntie Iris to the kids) was strapped in for the ride, the round robin of gossip and guffaws, the night spent at one sister's house, the next night at the other's—each believing herself the better hostess and wanting Iris to agree—the phone handed round the room as everyone said "Merry Christmas" to sister number four in Minnesota, snowed in with a husband, three sons, and a Border collie that was always herding everyone. And every year a drama: their brother's on-again-off-again with his kooky girlfriend; their mother's refusal to exercise ("Oh kids, can't you do it for me?"); the game of hearts ending in uproar when one sister shot the moon three hands in a row. Iris made small escapes, and as she was eldest, and single, no one said anything. During an afternoon session of Monopoly (a tedious game won by dumb luck that Iris wouldn't play), and knowing her mother wouldn't mind, she went looking for the old Christmas box in the basement. She found it on a gritty shelf in the furnace room, and took the ornament she'd treasured as a child.

You had to unwrap it carefully. It was a Nativity scene set in a hollow egg—mother, father, and child made of tiny wood spools and floating within on a cloud of spun glass. The color of the egg was palest green—the color, Iris imagined, of heaven on earth. She remembered when her parents brought it home from a trip to the Loop, where it had no doubt come from Marshall Field's. They were always bringing beautiful things home from Field's. She was enchanted by the egg, its magical containment, creation within creation, and said even then, "I want this ornament someday." One Christmas, when she was maybe thirteen, she unwrapped the egg, held it up, and thinking herself extremely clever said, "Hey Daddy, which came first, the Christian or the egg?" He thought it clever too, she could tell by the leap in his dark eyes, and that little movement he made at the corners of his mouth, that little catch just before a wide smile broke, and he challenged her in return, "If you can make that joke you can tell me what *you* think." And so, in her midthirties, with no one looking or probably caring, three generations distracted by Chance and Park Place, Iris packed the ornament into her suitcase.

The Christian or the egg. It *was* clever, and her heart ached with the shade of gray in the room that had not been there before.

It was at the end of a normal Christmas Day, Iris home from her first winter living in New York, that Iris, her sisters, and their young brother were brought into the family room for "a talk about life," and were told of their father's illness. A week later, Iris watched her parents welcome their closest friends for a New Year's Eve dinner, one of the elegant, intimate parties they did so well. When midnight struck, Iris was alone in the kitchen drying crystal glasses by counter light, darkness behind her. She heard New Year's cheers from the dining room, the comforting shrieks and inflections of longtime family friends. And then her father appeared in the kitchen. So smiling and hale and handsome, so salt-and-pepper trim in his tuxedo—he was looking for her, his eldest. He came to her with arms open and wordlessly they hugged. He just wrapped her in his arms in his fitted black jacket, an embrace that said I love you, I'm proud of you, always. It was a long moment, their whole lives as father and daughter caught up, her heart bursting to be brave and not break down. And then he returned to his party. Iris, these many years later, still felt held by that memory. The closeness and darkness. The grace. His beginning to say good-bye.

"Where are you?" Iris asked softly, then gave her head a shake.

She went to the window and shoved it up, letting the Manhattan cold meet the warm tree. More music! she thought, and put on her CD of Mozart arias, a recent gift from one sister. Iris stood back, took a sip of red wine, and surveyed the tree, which was glittering like a lady dressed for the opera. At that moment Elisabeth Soderstrom launched into *"Porgi, amor"* with a voice like antique silver, not unlike the garlands that shivered on the tree. Iris slid the town house window down a few inches.

She had the last set of ornaments to unpack, her latest collection and one she couldn't quite explain to herself—the blown-glass birds. These she kept in a biscotti tin, each wrapped in white tissue paper. The first she'd bought by accident, one of four ornaments in a little box she'd found on a weekend trip to Newport. The dealer told her it was the oldest in the box and really the best of the bunch. To Iris it looked like a crude silvery-pink submarine with a hole for a tail, a little upward squiggle for head and beak, and two wads of brackish tinsel wired where wings should be. When she got home, however, the more she looked at the bird, the more striking its elegance. Soon Iris was buying birds only. It made sense, after all, to have a tree full of birds. She found them with fantails of spun glass and for feet, metal clips, so they could sit on the branch as if just landed. She found regal oystery-green swans with three-pointed crowns, and jewel-toned peacocks, also with crowns (her mother's maiden name, in Hungarian, was Peacock). As she unwrapped each bird, she reassessed it, thinking this one is more beautiful then I realized, or, this one seems too fancy now, I'll pass it on. The birds she loved best were abstractions like the first, stylized like hieroglyphics, and floating within tangles of tinsel that might be wings or nest, as if the two could be the same thing. Could they? Wasn't life the nest or the flight? Was she holed up? Or flying away?

Iris forced herself to begin placing the birds, but even with the music turned up, the room was still. Her birds weren't lifting her as they had last year. Even as she climbed the ladder with her adored first bird, she thought, "I'm like you, stuck in old tinsel," then had to smile at such gloom. She took a deep breath, but her throat thickened anyway. The music ended, leaving Iris thoroughly alone on the ladder. She reached for a perfect bough, and as she leaned in to place the bird the scent of balsam sailed over snow-deep decades, a fragrance full of Midwestern winter, Christmas Eve, and sleep with dreams of morning—and all together the colored tree lights squeezed to star points then blurred. Iris felt tears on her cheeks, Iris who never cried.

I want this ornament someday.

Someday was calling her. And she had no idea how to answer.

Row J

Lana ran her eyes down the long row to her press seat, J-128, dead center. There was Fernanda, already sitting, her head cocked back at that familiar, questing, aggressive angle. It was 7:56 and Lana had to forge in, there were people waiting, impatient, behind her. She could feel her heart skiffing against her chest. You Cannot Run Away, she decreed to herself, her deep dismay shading into panic. Oh why did we have to be seated together?!

They hadn't spoken for two weeks. Not since the day after that night, that Sunday night when Lana got home from a weekend away with Megan.

It was Megan's idea, a spur of the moment decision to meet up on that first dull weekend after the new year—up in the snowy Berkshires, a midway point between them. It was fun, just the two of them poking into little shops, cappuccinos in the afternoon, doing the holiday postmortem: Megan's endless in-laws, Lana and Sam's first tree, Livia getting all hoity-toity in Kenilworth. And they'd talked a lot about Fernanda, irony of ironies, how everything was such an emotional battle for her, and how Lana, though weary of the Sturm und Drang, admired Fernanda's bravery in these battles, the way she faced the Bosch-like beaks of her personal demons. Perhaps Lana had been too proud of her position as guardian angel. Because overnight she was a fallen angel.

Lana had returned home from Massachusetts around five P.M. She and Sam were now renting a lovely old prewar on lower Fifth Avenue at Eleventh Street (no more the Dread Walk), but she still didn't like this hour, the weekend sifting away like the last sands in an hourglass, the coming work-week building into a huge drift. Sam's cat Spiffy arched her back against Lana's ankle as she let her bag slide to the floor, which Spiffy then sniffed. Where was Sam? Lana found him napping in the darkening bedroom. She snuggled in next to him—he gave her a groggy kiss—and felt happy and sad at once, happy she had Sam and sad because, well, she had always felt small on Sundays.

But the nap had a softening effect on the sadness, and seemed to lengthen the velvet interim between day and night. When Sam woke they didn't make love, just gossiped quietly, her head on his shoulder, and decided to make spaghetti for dinner. When they went through the apartment turning on the lights it was festive and cozy and golden. After dinner, Sam went to his study to do whatever (having a study was his one stipulation for moving in together), and Lana settled in to watch *Masterpiece Theatre*. And then the call came.

It was around nine-thirty and Fernanda's voice was high-flying, with that steel edge she could get when aggrieved.

"I was at the ballet today," she snapped, "and Rene showed me your article in *The Atlantic* and I always thought it was odd that *you* never showed it to me—for the whole month of December! Now I see why."

Gone the warm womb of PBS and Edwardian England. Gone the living room around her.

"It's this *huge piece.*"

Lana's mouth went dry.

"And you told me it was only a couple hundred words."

This was true. Lana had downplayed the scope, okay, the length, of the essay to the point where she was, yes, lying (her father's "jiggle the truth" was ringing in her ears). She'd been afraid to tell Fernanda it was a big piece, afraid for the friendship, because she knew Fernanda would resent that it was Lana who got the posh assignment and not she. Everything was fine as long as Lana remained second. Lana was the sensible one. She did not outshine her elders, or as Fernanda no doubt thought, her betters. Lana saw now she had only delayed the inevitable. In trying to be sensitive to Fernanda's feelings, she'd been sneaky. She should have told the whole truth.

But why should she have to write this piece under a black cloud? And since when did she have to report to Fernanda or anyone? Lana had worked long and hard all these years, and she had talent too. And it just so happened that Lana's talent went down easier than Fernanda's. It was one of the truths of New York that you learned within months: the most gifted didn't always prevail. They might be too complicated for the market, or too tender; or their talents not properly packaged, or controlled. Fernanda had gotten her chances in her first years here. And she had sabotaged herself in Fernanda fashion, turning in lengthy polemics she wouldn't have printed in her own magazine. Now Lana was having her chance.

"But that's nothing compared to the *bigger betrayal*," Fernanda said. "And you, Lana, of all people."

"But what have I done?" Lana cried, unable to keep defense out of her voice. You never, ever won in defensive mode, you only sounded weak and boy, did she sound weak now. Fernanda, hearing fear, bounced on.

"You stole my idea. You used my idea—*used me*. You stole my idea and sold it for *money*." She made the word "money" sound like a sin. Lana was in adrenal spasm. She was trembling.

"Whaaaat?" was all she could say.

"Plagiarism." The word shot through Lana, a word she never dreamed would apply to herself. "You know which line I mean," Fernanda blazed on, "the one about *Nutcracker* being a Christmas psychodrama."

"Fernanda," she appealed, "I know you've called it a psychodrama, but in my article I was asking what *kind* of psychodrama. I spun it out. You never did. I went to Tchaikovsky's diaries and letters. And I—"

"It was my line and you took it from me."

A line? It wasn't even a line, it was an observation, a Fernanda toss-off ("Yet another Tchaikovsky psychodrama"). Lana had lied about the length of the piece, but she had never hidden the subject. She'd brought it up with Fernanda at least twice.

"And if you had asked for it, I wouldn't have given it to you."

"But I did ask," Lana insisted. But had she? Or had mentioning it seemed like asking?

"And as far as I know you got the article on the strength of that line. My line."

That was snotty. Fernanda knew articles weren't assigned on the strength of a line. If anything, Lana "got" the article because the editor was impressed with her Saint Sébastien piece, which showed she could do a step-by-step analysis of a big work of art.

"It's not even a line," Lana said, knowing this would irritate but going in anyway, "everyone knows *Nutcracker* is one big subconscious. You should hear Dwight on the subject."

"I have a PhD and I don't need you—or Dwight Davis—to tell me what a line is. I feel like the composer in *The Red Shoes*. The one whose symphony gets ripped off."

The shock of the onslaught was bad enough, but to have one of her favorite movies flung back at her this way! At least, though, the trembling had stopped. It was now stone-cold misery. Walking through the room on his way to the kitchen, Sam gave Lana a questioning look, to which she shook her head gravely. He squeezed her shoulder.

Lana stopped defending and started apologizing. "I'm sorry you feel I took this from you," she said, which only inflamed Fernanda, who wanted an admission of guilt, not an offer of sympathy. Lana's sensibleness, stunned by the attack, began to kick in.

The truth was, Fernanda had been making Lana guilty for

months: for not calling enough, for not being available on Saturday nights, for moving in with Sam. Especially Sam. Fernanda had changed since the September move, as if she had been rewired and could no longer overlook little nothings—a message not returned until morning, an opposing view no matter how innocent. Lana felt herself absorbing little jabs of anger. And now this javelin. It was as if all Fernanda's issues with possession and power were gathered in that great heave, the word "plagiarism." In one of those long phone silences in which you hear the blackness of the universe, Lana's own words came back to her. With odd bravado she had said to Megan, "I know it will be my turn to fall from grace someday." Who'd have guessed that day would be the next day— TODAY.

An hour went by, and the conversation—circling, halting, flaring—finally ended with Fernanda calling a recess, saying she would be waiting to see what Lana did next. Exhausted and sick at heart, Lana placed the whole thing in Sam's lap, who thought the fight "high school" and the accusation absurd. "Even if you didn't ask," he said, "intermission chat is not intellectual property." As they fell asleep he stroked Lana's hand, and her heavily beating heart—Was I wrong to use her term? Is Fernanda right?—eventually slowed.

The next morning Lana woke with a start, daylight splashing the walls, and fell right back into her anxiety spiral: Fernanda's going to take me to court, I'm going to be labeled a plagiarist, Lana Prynne, *The Scarlet P.* There was no worse charge against a writer—it could follow you forever. Lana felt frightened, felt that Fernanda had been waiting for something like this, wait-

ing to pounce. Oh well, she thought, the bottom line is, I have
to do something.

Lana got to the office early, around eight. She wanted to call
Dwight. In the worst way she wanted to call him, but she knew
what he would say: "You've watched her fight with other people. Did you really think it wouldn't happen to you?" She
would hear him blowing out smoke—"talk about Christmas
psychodramas." She knew he would be blasé because she had
already intimated that things with Fernanda were increasingly
touchy and he'd hooted with mirth. They were eating at the
fried-egg dive near Lincoln Center, and he didn't look that
hot—thinner, tired—but her news perked him right up.
Dwight took a dim view of female friendship. Actually, he took
a dim view of everything. "I hate gay men, I hate straight men,
and I hate women," he once said to Lana, who could only
answer "D-w-i-g-h-t" with about ten syllables in it. She knew
he cared for her, but she didn't call him now because as he had
told her many times before: on the slippery slopes you're all
alone. And Lana didn't call Megan either. It was too early in
the morning—she'd call Megan tonight—and anyway, it might
seem petty to Megan. Lana had got herself into this, she'd
have to get herself out.

Instead of calling anyone, Lana practiced what she was
going to say, then at nine she called Fernanda.

"I think you're right that I didn't actually ask you about
'psychodrama,' " Lana said. "I just talked about using it. I just
assumed it was okay, 'cause you didn't say anything, but I
shouldn't have assumed. Maybe you felt too awkward to say
anything. If that's what happened then I was wrong."

"Thank you," Fernanda said. "I appreciate that."

Fernanda then admitted she did remember Lana talking about it (which Lana heard with deep relief, and thanked Fernanda for in return). Still, Fernanda wasn't sure it was enough. She said, "It would be better if you don't call me. I have a lot to think about."

So here they were, at the theater where they had met a year ago, first wary, then inseparable, and now . . . what? Walking the plank. Lana braved the gauntlet of knees leading toward the center. Fernanda bent her head to her program, and the lights came down as Lana sat down, sparing them both. The ballet was pink and pirouetty, but Lana, oppressed by that profile to her left, was sitting so stiff, her head so still, there was no continuity in what she saw—it was just weather in tutus. The minute the curtain calls ended, Fernanda was up and out. One ballet down, two to go.

Lana timed the first intermission well, coming in late again. But both of them miscalculated the length of the second intermission, for they headed in from opposite sides of the theater at the same time, saw each other across the way in the same moment, and refused to lose face by turning around.

"Hello, Lana."

"Fernanda," she nodded. Silence as they settled into their seats. Lana looked straight ahead at the curtain—an incredibly boring curtain. If she wasn't supposed to call Fernanda, she certainly wasn't going to start a conversation with her. She let her eyes wander up to the ceiling. It was latticed like a Fabergé egg.

"You know, Lana"—here we go, Lana could tell by the tone,

and she turned her face, but not her body, to Fernanda—"I've been thinking about what you said to me and it wasn't good enough. You didn't admit to taking anything." Fernanda was in full, contained, attack. "I want to hear you say the words. This friendship can't go on without it."

And what kind of friendship would it be then? Lana wanted to ask, but instead she said, "This again? I thought we reached an understanding on the phone, and now we're back at square one. I know I should have told you it was a big piece up front. I was wrong not to. But if you're asking me to grovel . . . I won't. That's not friendship."

"And what is? Stealing ideas from me so you can further your"—she put air quotes around the word—" 'career'?"

Lana gave her a long look. "I'm not going to go back over that psychodrama thing."

Fernanda stuck her nose in the air: "You should have known I didn't want you to use it."

"Yes"—Lana's blood was coming up—"yet again I was supposed to read your mind. I'm *soooo sick* of having to read your mind."

"But not sick of picking my brain. You know, this isn't your first steal."

Lana stared at her.

"Buffy the Vampire Slayer. I discovered her, and then you say you're going to write about her."

Lana's mouth fell open, then widened into a smile of amazement. "You saw it two episodes before I did—so that makes Buffy yours? She belongs to you? I don't get that. Why is she yours?"

Fernanda sat queenly, not deigning to answer as someone stepped over them—a purple skirt in front of their faces, and a brown purse bumping after. It snapped Lana back to the world around them, seats filling. Were people hearing this?! How did it sound? And if you saw them from up in the first ring, could you tell it was a fight? Lana straightened, and continued in a lower voice.

"You've really been storing it up, haven't you? So you could put me in the wrong. I had no idea you were so . . . so jealous."

Fernanda fluttered her hands in mock alarm. "Jealous! I'm really jealous of the person who thinks *Piers Plowman* is about farming. Who has to ask where Bosnia is." Lana never pretended she was a whiz at geography. "Or do you ask me these questions so you won't have to ask Sam? Wouldn't he be impressed?" She mimicked prettily, *"When exactly did World War II end? Was it '44 or '45?,"* then swung her voice down like an ax: "Pick someone else's brain, Lana."

There was no comeback to this. It was time to let it go.

"The fact is," Lana said low and fast, "you were looking for a way to end this friendship and you found it. It's always been about you. My loyalty, everybody's loyalty, to you. Well I won't be bullied anymore."

"Listen to yourself," Fernanda said, explaining Lana to Lana, "you're so angry. You think you aren't, but you are."

"And you're so small."

It was a mean thing to say but Lana didn't care, she was tired of being careful. It was dark again, the overture for the third ballet was about to begin, and they were just two heads in a sea of heads. So this is how it ends. Small and angry. Before she knew what she was doing, Lana leaned over and whispered, "I'm sorry, I never meant for this to happen."

"I'm not sorry," Fernanda said airily. "I feel better now."

And it was true. Fernanda wasn't just alive in battle, she was at home in its aftermath, that bitter, flattened landscape most people fear. It was just another living room to her, with broken glass. Now she'd be waiting and grateful for the next infatuated friend, and they'd redecorate together.

"Oh Fernanda"—Lana knew only too well—"you always do."

f(light)

Iris had just about had it with gallery girl. She knew it wasn't
politically correct to think of her as a girl. After all, this woman
owned the gallery. She was slim and intellectual, her black hair
smoothed back into a chignon tight as a tennis ball (a chignon
that never failed to impress Iris). She spoke in slim, hushed,
smoky tones—like a Bennington girl at a French film—and
wore slim, hushed, smoky cashmeres. She was convincing—
always convincing you of her taste, her ardor, her ambition to
be searchingly, aesthetically, right. And who was to say she
wasn't right? Her gallery—**flow**—was the hottest new space
west of Chelsea (way west, it was practically in the river). She
put herself on the map on *Charlie Rose*, when she said "Post-
modernism is puerile! A baby reaching for whatever bobs by."
It didn't hurt that she was glossy as a grackle, with a China doll

face. Charlie never leaned so far over his round table. She said, "My gallery is called **flow** because that is the state to which we all aspire. I show work that has reached intense equilibrium, the incandescence between innocence and experience, muscle and mind"—and then she laid her long ivory fingers on Charlie's big hand—"between nine-to-five, Charlie, and the sublime." He was all hers. "In other words, Charlie, I'm obsessed with that moment when craft fluoresces, transcends. I'm haunted by the guild arts—stonecutting, metallurgy, even plaster work—which are in such danger of disappearing. You know, when so much art is sham and careerism, we must listen for the music of the workroom. Have you ever noticed, Charlie, *the beauty* of the manhole covers in Manhattan?" Her name was Emily Edwards, but to Iris she was gallery girl. It was a way to keep that fantastic push at bay.

It all happened so fast. Well, slow, then fast. It began more than a year ago, that day in March when Iris went for a run in Gramercy Park and decided to make a lamp shade from branches. It wasn't that she was tired of silk. She would never be tired of silk. It had given her a living. But the bare branches in the park that day, they seemed to point the way, a path to another world.

She didn't begin immediately with the branches. She was still in the thinking stage and knew only too well how too impulsive a start can kill a project. She reined in her eagerness, channeling that energy into the eight sconce shades she was just finishing, which she delivered COD, a neat three thousand dollars (one thousand for taxes, one thousand for Keogh, one thousand for regular savings, the new black dress would have to wait). She bought a Peterson Guide—*The Trees of North America*—which helped her not at all. Then she took herself to Central Park early the next Sunday, and was struck as always by nature's elegance, its winter palette of tarnished silver and soot black, bleached green lichen, peridot green moss, ferns stiff and rusty, and brown puddles frozen pallid. She walked along, picking up fallen boughs and twigs, testing them for pliancy (not very), and dropping the more interesting ones into a lavender Bergdorf's shopping bag. Because of the cold the park was deserted, except for runners puffing by, little engines-who-could in gumball-colored fleece. They made Iris feel slow and eccentric, a wool coat picking up sticks. Yet when she saw a smudge of blue near a root she scrambled like a child, straightened up with a feather in her glove, a dusky blue with black stripes—bluejay?—and decided this was a good sign, she could go home. Besides, her toes were cold.

She started small—a sconce frame to which she glued the twigs from Central Park, placing them artfully, until she held before her the hut of a demented troll. This was not what she had in mind. Iris had to rethink the metal frame—either play the twigs off that rigid grid, or get rid of the grid altogether, which meant making her own frame (otherwise, how would it attach to the lamp?). I'll try one other thing today, thought Iris, who knew it could take some time before she figured out what she was doing. Saran Wrap? No. She went into the bottom drawer, pulled out a piece of bubble wrap, and wound it once around a second sconce frame, taping it just loose enough so the frame could slide out. This time, she was going to glue the twigs to each other, let *them* hold the shape, frameless. But how to start?

She positioned a twig—one that looked like a small hand—against the bubble wrap with her thumb, then let it drop. She went for a needle and thread. Lord I hate this getting up and down! She stitched the hand to the bubble wrap (it didn't matter that she punctured two bubbles), then positioned the second twig upon it, a dab of glue at every point they touched, then held it with her fingers. Her lips pressing together, she let the curve and splay of each twig suggest its placement, leaving them a bit airier, for a spidery look, but not too airy, or the bulb would glare. It went slowly, a twig at a time, spaced by minutes for the gluing, minutes in which Iris configured the next twig. She knew it should set overnight, but she couldn't wait, an hour would have to do. She went to the corner for coffee, where she anxiously flipped through an old *Elle Decor*, bored with everything that already existed.

Iris was prepared to be disappointed, because so often the idea in one's head couldn't be made to work in reality, but when she returned to the shade and snipped the threads, the frame and then the bubble wrap slipped free like sections of a space capsule, leaving her with a strange tracery of tree in her hand, something like those carmelized-sugar cages beloved of French chefs. "A wood near Athens" Iris said to herself, thinking of the setting for *A Midsummer Night's Dream*. She held it over a clear forty-watt torpedo bulb and the little thing threw mighty shadows up and around. Maybe too much light was coming through. It might need a discreet lining of gauze. But it was . . . speaking. It was a start. Iris named it Oberon. As for the troll hut—so homely—Iris decided she'd give it to Deena, just for the fun of seeing her sputter up a "thank you." It was, still, an Iris Original.

In the weeks that followed Iris portioned out the mornings for her twig shades, from eight to eleven. By spring she'd become a regular at the florist's, bringing home bunches of forsythia and curly willow and whatever interesting new thing had come in, discussing fine points of drying, wiring (she was now attempting larger shades), and flammability with a loquacious young salesman who himself looked made of curly willow. And yet she found she was drawn back to the parks, longing for the hunt. With Deena in tow, she went to The Ramble in Central Park (where Deena nearly fell off a small cliff, so avidly was she pointing at a rat in a ditch—"a rat, look, a rat"—to which Iris responded by yanking Deena back by the collar, handing her the bag of branches, and saying, "but unfortunately not your rich rat. Now look for gnarls"). Iris made trips to Riverside Park, where walking north toward Columbia she sneakily clipped fine sprays from the tops of bushes. Though she had never done—and would never do—a Hamptons share (just a little too much proximity to other people's intimacies, their sounds behind doors), she couldn't resist a Monday-through-Thursday in Sag Harbor in late August, a house open between weekends. She spent an hour each morning, her pants tucked into her socks, sleeves to the wrist, in the undeveloped lot next door, a meadow growing into a forest. She braved ticks and spiders in pursuit of treasure: the smear of guinea hen feathers left by a dog attack, milkweed pods spilling their seeds, flowers so tiny and meticulous they seemed conceived within the wrong end of a telescope.

In the workroom, however, Iris was pitiless about the things she'd gathered. The cult of dried field flowers, ashes of roses, all that musty sentimentality, that Toad Hall coziness, well it was another order of—what to call it—lifestyle? Kitsch? She was after something else, within reach but invisible, in the world but beyond the world. She kept returning to bare branches.

By November Iris had a suite of shades that were like nothing she'd ever seen. Each was distinct. Each she named. There was Titania, a sort of upside-down tulip shape in which Iris had worked eight lacy branches in the manner of a conventional spoke frame, the filigree at the end of each branch creating eight scallops along the bottom. She lined this with layers of moth gray tulle, pulled and twisted like old cobwebs.

Desdemona was made from stripped weeping willow branches that Iris swept in a spiral around an elongated onion shape. She left the tips trailing at the bottom, like loosened hair, the way weeping willows do.

Rusalka—Iris had to trek down to SoHo to find silver birch for Russian Rusalka.

Rapunzel was made with hawthorn branches run vertically around a long, slim, cylinder, an almost sixties shape, like a tower. Iris turned the thorns sideways, so the light would catch them in silhouette and they would suggest bricks or footholds—for the Prince to climb. Rapunzel was lined with a green taffeta darkened by black warp threads, the green of a spinach leaf.

Merlin took the cone shape of a sorcerer's cap. It was made from the gnarls and joints of oak branches glued together like a puzzle—no mean feat—and lined in a fine copper mesh that glinted. Indeed, constructing Merlin was like constructing a spell strong enough to hold him. Iris loved this shade especially, because it took twice as long as the others, and because she loved the lines from Tennyson that inspired it, the lines when Vivien traps Merlin in a tree:

> Then, in one moment, she put forth the charm
> Of woven paces and of waving hands,
> And in the hollow oak he lay as dead,
> And lost to life and use and name and fame.

Does anyone read Tennyson anymore? Iris wondered. In delight she recited, "Of woven paces and of waving hands." Oh the magic in those words. Was I, Iris thought, a bit of Vivien to Erich? She imagined herself pacing around him in their Society Hill living room, wishing him conventional—which was to him "as dead." Or, she sighed, maybe we just all trap each other.

Iris couldn't keep these shades in her workroom. It would be madness to have sticks and thorns near her expensive silks. No, Iris "did her branches" on the living room table, then hung or propped them in a walk-in closet off her front door. This was a dingy space where Iris had stored things she was saving "for the country house": an old pastry table wedged in dangerously sideways, two quaint wrought-iron chairs, a square tuffet with its stuffing falling out. But really. *The country house?!* Iris didn't even own this apartment. What was she thinking? She called in The Salvation Army, donated everything but the tuffet (it would be chic redone in stripes), and the newly emptied space became a little gallery with an audience of one—Iris. Nevertheless, the pull-out-put-back of materials every morning was tedious. One day, in the pre-Thanksgiving work rush, having been taken out for air, Merlin was accidentally left out.

"What is this?" called nosy Kiki Pollard with rising interest, having wandered into the living room while Iris was packing up a commission. You're all hounds, Iris thought. She hurried into the living room, saw Kiki hovering over Merlin, and went to him protectively.

"I'm experimenting with new materials."

"Are there more? Because if there are I'd like to see them. I'm doing a study for a bachelor—sort of Arts and Crafts meets modern. I've been looking for a fixture, a hanging lamp to float between the desk and the bookshelves. This branch thing could do the trick, hanging from a copper chain."

Kiki was right. It should hang.

"This is fantastic!" Kiki was getting excited. "No really. I think I have to have it."

Iris explained, "This took almost a month to make. It's one of a kind."

Kiki Pollard, so striking with her great gray eyes and pale cinnamon hair (so pale it was almost pink), could be a pain, always trying to wheedle extras, always saying, singsongy, "I'm a very good client, after all." But she could also be dear, forever sending Iris invitations to Philharmonic fund-raisers and such. Iris looked at Merlin—so beautiful she couldn't believe she'd made him, so patiently waiting. She didn't want to part with him. He was hers. But Kiki was waiting, and what could it hurt to test the waters? She fixed her hazel eyes on Kiki's glamorous grays, and said carefully, without give, "It's called Merlin. It's the sorcerer trapped in his spell." She doubled the price of her pagoda shade: "He's eight thousand dollars."

Seriously silent, Kiki focused her soul on Merlin. She took a step toward the shade, then asked, "May I examine it . . . him?" They turned the shade together, Iris's hands supportive underneath, and after a few soft nods, Kiki said, "Can I see him lit?" Iris placed Merlin over a bare bulb, and clicked it on. Kiki answered with an extravagant sigh.

"He's casting a spell as we speak!" Her checkbook was out. "We're talking stock-options money. It's going to make that room. I want to take it now. But no tax. Is it signed?"

It was—with a new symbol Iris had come up with upon finishing Merlin: a capital I inside the outline of an eye, like a hex sign. Iris stood for a second, not moving, trying on the idea— her Merlin, this cone of copper, his brain blazing, hers no more. Kiki laid her hand on Iris's arm.

"That's what artists do, Iris. They let the work go."

The next day, on her way to the bank, Iris could hardly believe the check in her pocket. She broke it down in her mind: three thousand for taxes, two thousand for Keogh, fifteen hundred for regular savings (rent was a waste, she needed to *own* an apartment)—*and fifteen hundred for a splurge.* The black Beene sheath! The Walter Steiger slingbacks! Or maybe that rock-crystal ball watch she'd seen on Twenty-fifth Street and couldn't stop thinking about—circa 1910, fifteen jewels, the circumference of a nickel! Of course, she would have to wait for the check to clear, but it was a windfall. A small windfall. But enough to disorient Iris, to make her feel fated, strangely more vulnerable, not less.

And the loss of Merlin was odd too. When she bought the ball watch—with its ghostly white face shimmering through the crystal dome on one side, and a tiny windup infinity of silver wheels and gold cogs locked in and ticking beneath the crystal dome in back—she thought it would always remind of her of the shade that had paid for it. But no. It reminded her of her father. It was the kind of object he would have loved. The kind of thing he would have bought for her.

Iris began Aurora in early December. It was a few days after the night she decorated her tree, that desolate night when she started crying near the ceiling, making it hard to see coming down the ladder (and why bother? who cared if she ever came down?). The holidays had never hit her like that before, and as lovely as the tree was, she couldn't enjoy it, she could hardly look at it. Yet there it stood, eight feet tall, glass birds motionless, filling the living room with a vast quiet. Aurora, a shade evoking *The Sleeping Beauty*—it was to be a fairy curtain of vines lined with lilac—fell prey to false starts, the vines too flimsy, the shape not true, the lilac silk only pretty, insipidly pretty, ugly, mauve and old-lady, nothing like spring, Iris hated it, she jammed it in the trash. Anyway, Iris had no feeling for spring—raw light, cracking ice, rivers of slush and mush—she'd never liked spring and just now she loathed it. The Christmas tree, serene witness to all this, rebuked her too. Why would you do a spring subject, its presence seemed to ask, in winter? Iris pulled out the bag of thick thorned vines that had not worked for Rapunzel. She began to wind and weave, the vines taking possession of her—or of themselves— pricking her fingers with their thorns, and becoming—it took two whole days—a dense veined tangle before her, a furious knot that needed no lining, that could hold one hundred years. She realized she had made a kind of nest. Only it was bottomless. She called it Bramble. Under the blue-green branches of her cold Christmas tree, Iris began, feverishly, to make nests.

At the end of the following February, on a Monday morning, Iris received a phone call.

"This is Emily Edwards. I'm trying to reach Iris Biddle."

"This is she."

"Ms. Biddle, I own **flow** gallery. I was at Joel Skelly's on Saturday night, and I saw a hanging lamp you made. Out of oak branches. I'd like to know if you have any more of these?"

"Oh Ms. Edwards, I do apologize. I'm not taking any new orders until June. But if you—"

"Excuse me," the voice cut in, "I don't think I've made myself understood. I don't want to buy your lamps. I want to sell them. The piece I saw at Joel's was technically amazing. I've never seen anything like it. It was so"—the voice paused for effect—*"sentient."*

"Oh," Iris said, not sounding as surprised as she probably should have. She knew Merlin was magic.

"Your lamp embodies everything my gallery stands for. The moment when craft transcends into art. I'm always talking about 'incandescence,' and here is your work, literally, *incandescent.*"

Emily Edwards went on to explain what kind of work had been shown at **flow**, the superb coverage and sales, the ascent of her artists, then let her voice fall grave, "I would be honored if you would let me see more."

How could Iris say no? They made a date for the first Friday in March—a year almost, since beginning with the branches! When Emily Edwards stepped through the door, she was neat as a pin in lean cocoa cashmere, her chignon shining, her cocoa suede Blahniks pointy as a poodle's nose (Iris loved poodles, but she'd never liked brown ones). They shook hands and Iris led Emily, surely not yet thirty, into the living room where she had a small stepladder ready, and an extension cord.

"I'm going to have to hold each one aloft for you," Iris said, "because they should be shown hanging. Like chandeliers."

She brought out one shade at a time, in the order they were made, saying only the name from the stepladder, then switching on the light.

"All lampshades have two lives," Iris explained. "One with light, and one without."

Emily Edwards kept silent. When Iris brought out Bramble, Emily's mouth fell open.

"A breakthrough," she said as if to herself.

She sees it, thought Iris.

When the nests came out, bottomless brambles of whispery, lacelike hysteria, thickets of short sticks stained with pomegranate, blackberry; then nests with liver-spotted quail eggs, thrush eggs the color of faded turquoise, the eggs blown, placed in tangles, suspended inescapably in nest-walls of branch, of vine; and then the nests with small guinea hen feathers, and breast feathers of the mourning dove Iris found dead on the sidewalk, feathers varnished onto the branches like fingerprints, like shadows—Emily was still as stone, a manicured hand knuckled to her mouth.

"They're ruthless," she finally said. "Aren't they?"

Iris nodded yes.

"They're traps—self-possessed, self-absorbing. Birth, copulation, and death all caught up and"—she searched for the word—"compressed. Do they have titles?"

Iris shook her head no.

"Of course they don't. They're like the poems of Emily Dickinson, if she used sticks instead of words."

Emily Edwards stood up.

"So," she said, "we have to be ruthless too. I came here wanting to do a show of Merlins, but the nests blow everything else away. The early shades are 'about' art. They're decorative. The nests are life and death. I could put both in the gallery, but the contrast would confuse people. So the show is the nests. And Bramble—I see Bramble hanging center in the space, in a shaft of light, with the rest revolving around it." She paused, thinking. "As for the art shades, we'll photograph them for a notebook of your early work. They'll sell like hotcakes—to people afraid of the nests but who want a piece of you."

Then everything happened fast. Contract signed, Iris always seemed to be penciling in meetings with the design team, talking to the PR guy, riding west in cabs, barely keeping up with her silk shade business. Emily wanted Iris to write out a detailed bio and CV, no flick-of-the-wrist if you'd never done them before.

And Emily wanted Iris to make another Merlin, just in case Skelly decided not to let Merlin hang in the show.

"But I thought you didn't want the decorative shades in the show," Iris said, thinking back and ahead to how difficult Merlin was to make.

"I know I said that, but Merlin is special. I want him near the entrance, as an example of your early work, to show what the nests evolved out of."

"But I can't make another Merlin. There's only one."

Emily gave her the fish eye. "Did Mondrian do just one grid? Monet, one water lily?" Then added soothingly, "We'll call it Merlin Two. Think of it as the sorcerer splitting into apprentices."

It was difficult getting around Emily. Not only was she creamily controlling (and Iris was no slouch in the control department), she had an instinct for sensibility, her finger on your pulse, which was actually irritating. So it would be Iris and Deena back in Central Park.

Then Emily wanted Iris to make a list—call in every marker—of every person she knew in social, art, and media circles. That was a horrifying proposition.

And Emily, at seven on a Monday night, just as Iris was leaving for the opera, wanted her to look at a fax she'd just sent, so they could sign off on the show's title: **(f)light** or **f(light)**? It was at this point Iris began to think of Emily, ungratefully, as G.G. (gallery girl with poodle shoes).

"I don't understand why you would put parentheses around the f," Iris said. "Why emphasize the letter f?"

"Tom"—G.G.'s snappish design chief—"argues that it's like the lightbulb around the filament."

"Isn't that a stretch?" Iris asked. "I like the second one. If the parentheses are a lightbulb, then light should be inside. And the word 'light' is *inside* the word 'flight.' It's more logical." Though saying it sounded sophomoric.

"Tom feels strongly, and I agree with him, that the first is more kinetic, more like flicking on a light: *ffff*-light. He thinks it has more edge."

Iris hated being late to the Met. She hated sitting in that awful train-station-like room with the video screen, where latecomers waited for the first intermission. Iris was feeling "more edge" with every minute.

"Emily, I really must go. I never thought it needed parentheses in the first place. But if it's one or the other, I think it should be the second one. Tell Tom I respect his opinion, but *ffff*-light is more him than me. And it is my show. Isn't it?"

It was going to be a fall show, opening in September, and Iris was surprised by how excited she was. Could the nests really sell at those prices? And would people understand them? Or think she was bats?

Iris finished Merlin II in late April. She knew exactly what she was doing this time, so it went smoother and faster. He was technically better than the first Merlin, a little taller, and the oak knots fitted tighter. But he was a younger Merlin, not ancient, waiting, like the first. The spell was never the same the second time around. When Iris delivered Merlin II on the first day of May, Emily—looking the little ivory empress behind her black lacquer desk—informed her that both *Town & Country* and *Vanity Fair* were doing small articles, so interviews and two shoots would have to be set up in the next few weeks.

"It will be a swarm of stylists," Emily warned, "but it's kind of fun to have all those hands buzzing around you." And then she said, "Dress for fall, no bright colors. We want sleek, serious, modern. They'll want to play up the Main Line, the Biddle name. I'll try to be there. But if I'm not, no costume drama. No pearls and white gloves."

Iris liked the idea of white gloves—but saw Emily's point.

"And don't let those stylists put you in trendy either. No Prada. Or anything Japanese. Well, Yojhi's good. But no weird Rei!"

Yes, yes, thought Iris, who knew perfectly well how to present herself, thank you very much.

"That necklace you're wearing." Iris's ball watch was hanging on a silver chain, not long, as such watches were worn in their day, but shorter, over her heart. "It's so surreal. Magritte."

"Yes," Iris agreed, looking down her long, fine nose to admire it herself. "Isn't it wonderful?"

"It might work well in a photograph," Emily said, "if it's a close-up. *Town & Country* does close-ups. It could be quite Horst." Pleased just thinking about it, Emily stood up and leaned across the desk for a better look. "It's so unique. Where did you get it?"

Iris gazed down at the watch once more. "It was a gift," she said, turning it around to show the inner workings in back, "from my father."

An Hour of Your Time

When Lana got the assignment she called Deena. She felt funny about it. They hadn't talked in ages, maybe just twice since Deena helped Lana and Sam find the apartment at Fifth Avenue and Eleventh. Deena had gotten deep into past-lives therapy, mystic and histrionic healings taking place in other dimensions, and her conversation kept heading back to other eras (the here and now was boring). But this was a good reason to call. It would give Deena a chance to give advice, which everyone liked to do—not to mention, Lana needed advice. She dialed.

"Long Lost Lana!" Deena said with a spike.

"I know, I know," Lana said. "I'm terrible. But I've been out of touch with everyone. Part of it's moving in with Sam—I really haven't figured out the balance. Will you accept an apology?"

Lana was trying to get away from "I'm sorry," which she said so often and so automatically it was hardly sorry at all. You almost never heard the word "apologize" anymore. It was too abject in these days when no one wanted to admit that they were wrong. But it did sound better.

"All *riiiight*," said Deena, her Southern accent warming. "What's up? How's the apartment?"

"The apartment's great. We love it. But listen, remember how you've always been wanting me to meet Iris Biddle?"

"Yes. Why haven't we done that yet? You grew up practically next door to each other."

"Deena. Evanston and Barrington are at least an hour apart. Anyway, guess who I'm interviewing for my first *Vanity Fair* assignment?"

"*Finally*," Deena said. "Finally a real magazine."

It was that female thing, using a pat-on-the-back to deliver a zing. Lana ignored it.

"But guess who?"

"Who?"

Exasperated, Lana said, "*Iris Biddle!* Her debut exhibition at **flow** gallery."

Deena shrieked, then bubbled. "Can I be at the interview? I'll be the maid. I'll serve tea."

Lana was thinking how to say no nicely.

"I'm only kidding," Deena said. "And by the way, I helped with those things."

"You did?" Lana was dubious.

"I helped pick the branches, which isn't as easy as it sounds."

"So tell me again what Iris is like? How should I approach her? Give me tips."

When you got Deena to buckle down—*finally*—she was pretty sharp. She said Iris would be wonderful, "but two things. Take whatever she serves, tea, drinks. She's got a real bug about people coming over and just wanting water." (Yeah, Lana thought, you've done that water bit with me too, Deena.) "Also, she's sensitive about her divorce. The husband ran off to Africa—just left her—to dig for emeralds or something—*can you believe it?* I think he's in the Peace Corps now. She's weird about the whole Biddle thing. She sort of laughs at it, but not about him. So don't bring it up."

————

Lana had to bring it up. Her editor said explicitly, "We want to know about being a Biddle, the family, the marriage, did she know the Mayflower Madam, et cetera." Standing at the door of the town house on East Nineteenth Street, Lana was anxious to get it over with. She didn't like doing interviews—the fawning required, the squeezing out answers, the ceaseless worry over the tape recorder and whether the pause button was hit by accident. Lana rang the bell and was buzzed in immediately. She pulled out her notebook and wrote, "on the dot punctual," then headed up the stairs to the third floor.

When the door opened, big smiles and bashful hellos as Lana shook Iris's hand, unsure of how familiar they really were, each knowing about the other through Deena—indeed, knowing more than they should know, bits and pieces gathered over the years, like how Iris took ages to buy a new mirror for her bathroom on Nineteenth Street. "It was this old streaky thing with the silver comin' off," Deena said, "and I said, 'Iris, this mirror,' and she says, 'I like a mirror I can hide in.' Which is weird, don't ya think?" Or how Iris's upstairs landlords were always asking her to cat-sit just as they were leaving for the airport, so she couldn't say no, which infuriated Iris but amused Deena, who imitated Iris: "What if *I* were going somewhere? Then what would they do?" "Truth is," Deena said, "Iris doesn't go anywhere. She's married to those lamp shades."

The funny thing was, it all evaporated when you were face-to-face with the person. Lana had imagined Iris as lady of the manor, forbidding, tall, because of Barrington and Biddle and because Deena called her bossy. The woman who answered the door, however, was a fresh forty-one (the bio didn't mention Iris's age, but Deena did), with a posture that made her seem tall (Lana straightened right up), and large hazel eyes that took you in completely. She had haughty bones, yes, a bit like pictures of Babe Paley, especially the nose, and an aura of . . . aloofness? No. Reticence? No. Containment! She was dressed in an airy white blouse, collar turned up, made of curiously stiff thin silk ("gazar," Iris later informed her) and neat black cigarette pants. On her feet—sort of slipper shoes of bronze paisley lamé ("vintage Vivier," Iris later explained). Lana started talking.

"I'm so glad you suggested we do the interview here. I can't tell you how nerve-racking it is to do them in restaurants. Even the quiet ones are loud—clinking silverware, interruptions. This is so much better." She looked around the living room. "And so beautiful." It was a grand room—ten-foot ceilings, three big windows—made grander by long wall hangings, one on each side of the fireplace, ceiling-to-floor unfurls of antique silk alive with arabesques and butterflies, silver threads on a sky blue background, and gold threads on celadon, and all this against willow green walls. "Wow," Lana said, thinking "house-proud."

Iris motioned toward a loveseat and wing chair near the corner window. A lucite tea trolley of Art Deco design was waiting with service for two complete with finger sandwiches.

"Where did you find that?" Lana blurted, knowing it was unusual, twinging that her own place was so undone, the bedroom still in boxes. She and Sam had to get their act together.

"I designed it," Iris said, "and had it made. That's one of the amazing things about New York. You can find someone to make anything in this city."

They sat down.

Lana began futzing with the recorder—"testing, testing"—then set her notebook by her side and jotted "B. Paley / hazel eyes / swirling embroideries." Iris brought in hot water for tea.

"We have Earl Grey, blackcurrant, chamomile."

"Blackcurrant," Lana said, "to go with your branches."

Lana skimmed through the formative years. ("Childhood is boring," Sam always said. He read a lot of biographies.) And she'd learned to keep questions short.

"How does it feel to suddenly be 'An Artist'?"

Iris was pouring out second cups of tea with the precision of Edith Wharton. Watching—jotting without looking, "E. Wharton tea/Ellen Olenska??"—Lana noticed that Iris's hands had tiny coral cuts, like slivers. The nails were short; buffed, not polished. Iris caught Lana studying her hands and held one up between them, the way surgeons put up a hand for the glove.

"They're cuts from thorns." She let the hand down. "You think you're being so careful, and then you get stuck by one you didn't even see was there. And it's not like I'm not used to this. With silk shades, it's pins and needles that get you. I've tried wearing gloves, but it just doesn't work—you can't feel anything. The upside is, you can bleed on branches without ruining them."

There's my lead, Lana thought.

"But in answer to your question, it feels good. I mean, we all love attention. Still, I always thought my silk shades were art. Though most people would call them craft."

"That's one of those blurry differences, art or craft. But you did make a leap at some point."

"I leapt to new materials. But isn't that always the way? You let the materials speak? It's like what I was reading about Mozart—I just got a CD of *Così fan tutte*—and he had a soprano who could hit really low notes, so he wrote arias that go really low, which he hadn't done before."

Lana nodded. "It's such a great opera."

"It is," Iris said. "I just saw it at the Met last season—I'd never seen it before."

"In Chicago did you go to the Lyric?"

"Not for opera. My parents took us there when the ballet came to town, and then it stopped coming. I remember my dad driving us to Milwaukee to see American Ballet Theatre. He'd speed on that long highway." She was enjoying remembering. "This is when he had a Mercedes, and he loved that car. He said he was letting it out for exercise. We were terrified—I think he hit 105. Then he did get a ticket. And we were glad."

"But back to the leap. How did you get the idea for that?"

"I had bought a book of photographs by Josef Sudek, which are full of trees and branches. I can show it to you."

She was up, disappeared down the hall, and came back with the book. She laid it on Lana's lap.

"Open it anywhere," she said. "What I really love is his feeling of things waiting. A world that's dormant."

Dormant, Lana thought, such a beautiful word. She opened on a photograph called *Saint Vitus Cathedral, 1924–1928* and studied it. Stone, stillness, three looming interior arches, and through each, light shafts angled down from on high. The light was stiff like a wedding veil, so feminine, and so fierce.

"And one day, it was in winter, I was staring into the treetops, and I thought, why can't I use branches too? And I decided to try."

Lana kept leafing and found the photos of trees. They did seem to have a secret, a wisdom within.

"So Sudek was the touchstone?"

"Well, it was more like a refrain. For as long as I can remember—and I assume a lot of people feel this way—bare branches have made me feel so . . . forlorn. I wanted to try and use that."

Lana liked the way Iris's short dark hair brushed back from her temples in almost tailored waves.

"And had you always been obsessed with nests?"

Iris thought for a moment.

"I don't see myself as obsessed with nests. This is a development. To me, a lamp shade around a lightbulb is like a nest with an egg."

"So you never made a study of birds' nests?" Lana didn't

mean to beat this to death, but in interviews the more answers you got the better, so it never hurt to ask the same question two, even three ways.

"No. And I didn't look in any nature books because I didn't want to be influenced. I mean, I wasn't trying to knock off nature. I was trying for something else. The spirit—the spell of the branches."

"I look at the nests," Lana offered, "and to me they seem to be saying, in an abstract way, that the branch, the nest, and the feather are all one thing."

"Yes. The bird and the branch are one."

"Do you miss working with silk?"

"I still have my silk shade business, cut back a bit. So no, I don't miss it. But I must admit, there's such freedom when I'm working with vines and branches. It's like an escape."

Iris took a finger sandwich, her third. Lana had already chowed down five.

"Yet Emily Edwards calls them traps," Lana said.

"I can't explain them. And too much talk is killing, don't you think? When I do them I'm caught up."

That "killing" line was good. Lana glanced at the recorder to make sure the tape was turning. She returned her eyes to Iris, who was taking a sip of tea.

"Now," Lana said with a sway of regret, hoping to distance herself from these next questions, "I have some things the magazine wants me to ask."

Iris was looking at her.

"You can say 'no comment.' "

Iris kept looking.

"Is it true your former husband, Erich Biddle, left science to start an emerald mine and it was a scandal?"

"No. There was no scandal at all. But he did go looking for emeralds."

"Why emeralds?" Lana was mystified.

"It was baffling to everyone," Iris said, "and so . . . ridiculous-sounding."

Lana didn't say anything. She waited. A time-honored interview tactic.

"Erich had a doctorate in neuropharmacology," Iris said, stepping into the silence. "So you couldn't tell him anything about brain chemistry. Certainly I couldn't, though it's clear to me now he was just . . . dissolving. Anyway, a while ago I came across an article on gems, and it said emeralds, in ancient times, were thought to calm the soul and even cure madness. I'd never heard that before. And I don't think Erich knew it. Despite the family history with gems, you know, Bailey Banks and Biddle."

Of course—the jewelry store—Lana was fascinated.

"It made a kind of poetic sense to me. It fit him. He was trying to save himself. He was never like anyone else." Then Iris stopped, concerned. "You won't put this in the article?"

"No," Lana said, intoning toward the tape recorder: "That was off the record." She straightened up. "But now, on the record, are you still in touch with him?"

"Yes."

"Really?"

"He sends me funny postcards from Africa."

A good reporter would ask if he ever sent an emerald,

but what did it matter? Iris was being great. Why risk upsetting her?

"Deena said he's in the Peace Corps now."

"He has been for quite some time. In the field, but very high up."

Lana heard the pinch of pride in that answer. She wondered if Iris was still in love with the man. Shouldn't she have remarried in all this time? As far as Lana could see, Iris wasn't nutsy like so many New York women, though you couldn't always tell from the outside. What was wrong? Lana didn't like to think that people with nothing wrong could end up alone. She soldiered on to her crummy last question.

"Did you—do you—know the Mayflower Madam?"

"*Lifestyles of the Rich and Famous!*" Iris taunted, her eyes bright, almost more green than hazel. "I never met her—but I wouldn't have. That was a whole other wing. And Erich and I were off on our own—you know, the campus life. But it can seem that big old families have more folly. It's definitely more glaring when they do. Is that enough of an answer?"

Lana nodded. "Thanks." She set her notebook aside. Then leaned in, delighted it was done. "So have you talked to Deena lately?"

"Just the other day—to find out about you."

"Uh-oh."

"She said you were serious." Iris slid the last sandwich onto Lana's plate. "And a wonderful writer."

"Wow. That's really nice. I think I'm too hard on Deena sometimes."

"She can be trying. But she really does mean to be generous."

"But what do you think about that illness?" Lana was riding a fine line, not knowing how far Iris would go, how protective she was of Deena.

"It's very mysterious," Iris replied. "She always seems perfectly well to me. I mean, the energy it takes to run around town like that."

"She told me she was dropped on her head as a baby."

"Nooo," Iris cried, her smile surprisingly wide.

"Yes," Lana chirped. "That's why she feels off, her chakra's out of alignment."

"She never told me that," Iris said. "She probably didn't dare. I'm a doctor's daughter and she knows I'm leery of her therapies. I once called her doctor a quack, it was a slip, and she almost hung up on me."

"The story is"—Lana was a bit giddy on gossip—"she went home for Christmas, this was a year ago, gunning, just gunning. She actually confronted her mother. I'm sure the mother was dumbfounded. Anyway, Mom totally denied it and there were tears and recriminations. It totally backfired. Plus, now Deena can't say for sure she was dropped on her head."

"This conversation is just *crying* for a martini," Iris said, relaxed in her white silk wing chair, "if it weren't still so early. Now, it is true that babies often get dropped. Or fall. And no harm comes of it. My own sister was *horrified* when her son stood up in his high chair and fell out right on his head"—her finger drew an arc in the air—"like a dud rocket." They both started laughing. "But the fact is"—Iris was talking while laughing—"Deena has a perfectly round head"—she was girlish in laughter—"no dents anywhere."

"Okay," Lana said, thinking martinis would have been fun,

"head aside. Don't you find it annoying, not knowing if she's really sick?"

"I used to be baffled by it," Iris said. "But now I see it as a coping mechanism. It takes huge resources to be a single woman here, which I'm sure you know. And as you get older people start wondering about you, why aren't you married, what's wrong with you?"

Lana blinked, guilty.

"I think Deena uses the illness to hide in," Iris continued, "to escape all that. As long as she's on her quest to get well, those issues are kept at bay. And never mind everyone's expectations."

"Do you," Lana couldn't resist, "have a coping mechanism?"

"It's easy, isn't it—and fun—to analyze one's friends. I suppose I lean on the past too. I had a really happy childhood. But the luck of that, it can make you sort of, well, passive, later on. Like the bad things that happen when you're older are just the score being balanced, so you accept it. You say, but my childhood was so great. . . . But"—it seemed Iris had given this some thought—"maybe that's not the best thing to do." The room was cool, the north light reserved, even though it was sunny outside. "And what about you, Lana?"

It was always strangely pleasant to hear someone new say your name.

"I don't know. I just keep rolling along." The thing was, Lana no longer thought of herself as single.

"As for Deena," Iris resumed, getting up while Lana packed to go, "even if we knew exactly what was wrong, would that make her any easier to take in large doses?"

On that note, a merry gleam between them, they walked to

the door and shook hands once more. Then Lana asked, as she always did, "If I have any follow-up questions, would you mind if I call you?"

"Of course you can call. And I'll look for you at the opening."

———

Lana trotted down the stairs. It was ten of three. No matter how well an interview went, it was jail break getting out, getting your own life back. Unfortunately, Lana was expected at Dwight's at four—about six blocks west on Eighteenth Street. She didn't like to stack Saturdays like this, she liked to keep Saturdays for herself, but Iris said one and Dwight said four, and there it was, Lana had an hour to kill. She debated shooting home to Eleventh Street, but why go downtown for fifteen minutes, only to bounce right back uptown? She could browse at ABC, which was on the way to Dwight's—but it wasn't fun to browse when you had to keep looking at your watch. What she really wanted was a cup of coffee ("doing tea" was a treat, but tea itself was wimpy). When Lana got to Fifth Avenue, she pulled into the first coffee shop she saw and took a seat at the counter.

It was like slipping into old shoes. Chicago, New York, these coffee shops were all alike, from the fake-looking cakes in steel-and-glass cases to the sugar-slick Danishes under scratched plastic domes. All she needed was a *Kenyon* or a *Hudson* or a *Partisan Review*, ten extra pounds, a Brooks Brothers skirt that nagged at the waist, and she'd be back in Chicago, postcollege, pre-everything. How many hours over extra-light coffee? How many chef's salads on oval platters, the latest Saul Bellow propped plate-side, pages catching specks of dressing. Her favorite coffee shop, the Carnegie Deli in the Drake Hotel, no longer existed. Now that was Old Chicago, the most wonderful little room, tucked away from the Drake's ground-floor warren of pricey shops and restaurants. It was like being in a back pocket—you could feel massive Lake Michigan, that harsh slab of sky and water only a stone's throw away, pressing against the walls. But before you, the creamiest, chunkiest chicken salad, and chocolate shakes cold and thick with ice crystals. Gone now.

She'd come so far, and yet here she was in the same old coffee shop, the same bone-colored crockery before her. She'd just done her first interview for *Vanity Fair*, the most glamorous magazine in America, and here she was slurping joe from a stool. It was pretty neat though, that they had called her! She'd never dream of calling them. But one of the editors had read her *Atlantic* piece and thought it classy ("With that eye," the editor said, "you can write about anything"). Lana's piece on Iris was only 350 words, but she'd make it pop. She'd play Iris's old-world formality off her ferocious nests. There was something fairy tale about Iris, like a woman weaving her own tower of twigs, Rapunzel at one with the thorns. Maybe Lana could do something with the green in her eyes and the emeralds. Or maybe not. There was a shadow there. Maybe that's why she was alone. The husband gone, and all those cuts and pricks and pins. It seemed symbolic. The sacred wound. People did not let go of those wounds so easily. Lana wouldn't pursue that though. She'd keep to the quotes and the nests, which was more than enough. This was going to be fun to write.

And what would Fernanda think when she saw it? *If* she

saw it. It was five months since their fight in January, but it still made Lana queasy. At least she'd stopped contemplating the things Fernanda might be saying about her. And there was the upside—no more pressure to call, to guess, to flatter, to finesse. New York was a strange city. In the last year and a half Lana had lost two friends—both of whom believed she'd betrayed them. Had she? Little Lana from Evanston, Illinois? She understood how trying it must be to have a younger friend and colleague disagree with you, or gaining on you, or even passing you by. She understood that when she moved in with Sam, Fernanda felt distanced. In fact, it was Sam who said, "You did take something from Fernanda—yourself." Lana had pretended nothing was different after the move, pretended she wasn't tired of Fernanda's constant need and phone calls. But wasn't that also a kind of lying to Fernanda? A lie Fernanda saw through—and being her father's daughter, she would do the pulling away. Lana wished she hadn't called Fernanda "small." She meant it the moment she said it, but it wasn't true, or true only in that Fernanda was small like a child, with a child's need to test and reject, to control through testing and rejecting. Lana wished she could take it back. Still, Fernanda's attacks on her, the *vehemence* of them. Lana would never forget it—the length a person would go to, not to be left behind. She hoped she would never have to feel that way.

Lana had given Livia dispatch reports on what was happening at the time, but recently she'd called on a Sunday when her brother Tom happened to be there too, dropping off some family photos.

"It seems to be a pattern," Lana said. "Something about me makes these women angry. And I really try so hard not to make anyone angry."

"First, they tend to be older than you," Livia said. "Right? Which starts you off subordinate. Second, correct me if I'm wrong, they're divas. And you're not a diva. You don't have as much baggage."

Livia was the diva in the Burton household, though none of them had the heart to tell her so.

"And we all know what happens when you don't have as much baggage," Tom yelled from the background. Then Lana heard fumbling and his big voice was on the line: "You end up carrying their bags too."

"He's right," Livia called from behind.

"Okay kid"—Tom liked to solve problems—"what's the return on the investment? That's the question you need to ask." Tom was bullish in a brokerage firm, very can-do. "Remember that science project you did? Where you took two of the same plant and grew one in the sun and one in the shade. Remember how you identified with the spindly shady one?"

"Tom. That plant died."

"That's my point. You're not that kind of plant. You like shade. Remember how in nursery school, you sat under the table during your recital"—a famous family anecdote—"letting other people shine? You did that because it was the right light for the Lana Burton brand of photosynthesis."

"You make it sound like I'm using people."

"I do not make it sound that way. It's symbiotic. But obviously not anymore. You're ready for some sun. And while you're at it, kid, stop pigeonholing yourself as a critic. People hate critics. Do yourself a favor and call yourself a writer."

"Tom?"

"What?"

"Who's snorting in the background."

"Go ahead and change the subject. That's our new puppy, Dickens, a French bulldog. He burps, he farts, he wheezes. The kids love him. And now I've got to get him home. So here's Livia . . ."

There were endless theories, and in a way, endless truths. You formed them, you weighed them, you went on. Lana kept remembering something Fernanda had said during their last phone call, when Fernanda thanked Lana for her apology but said she wasn't sure "it was enough." It seemed to Lana that this was at the heart of every accusation and stand-off, every shoot of anger and pain, the question of what was or wasn't enough. Did any two people in the world measure it the same way? Enough?

Lana glanced at her watch. She'd leave in ten minutes. She didn't know how long she'd be at Dwight's, but if it wasn't too late, she'd stop afterward at Bed Bath & Beyond. Lana and Sam desperately needed new towels. When they moved in together he'd brought his navy blue with red stripes—ahoy matey!—and she'd brought her yellows, once frothy, now flat with use. Iris Biddle's apartment, those cool colors and shimmering silks, had made Lana feel the want of luxury. She'd begin with big, white, fluffy, bleachable towels. She'd charge them with their new joint credit card, and dump the blues and yellows.

Lana motioned for a refill. She added cream and sipped the hot, thin, pale, mellow coffee. Dwight had finally told her he'd tested positive, which she had suspected, given his weight fluctuations a while back. These days, with the drug cocktail, you didn't know anymore who was or wasn't. People were flourishing, and the cloud of gloom that had been hovering, pressing on the lives of every New Yorker whether they knew it or not, cared or not, had sex or not, had drifted off. The *Times* obit page, for ten long years a kind of Green Fields of France, was once again the province of the old. But suspecting was one thing. Hearing Dwight say it was another. Lana had not been equal to the moment—the sudden dark tunnel over the phone line connecting him to her. What was it she said? It troubled her to think of it.

"Oh."

She who worked daily with words. He had waited on the other end of the line, while her eyes adjusted in the under-world. "It's going to be okay though," she said. "It's not what it used to be." To which he said, "I know." Then they talked on, getting used to the new terrain—doctors, drugs, side effects. Dwight was tough, there was no doubt about that, already making jokes. At the end of the conversation, even though they didn't have a touchy-feely friendship, Lana said, "We . . . I . . . love you." And he said again, "I know."

Dwight was doing all right on the cocktail but he would have been doing better if he'd started sooner. Stubborn, secretive, and at the end of the day so alone, he had denied his symptoms and put off seeing a doctor. So he was up and down, but thank God getting stronger. And the good news was, he'd just gotten a book deal—an impressive six-figure advance for a critical biography of Baryshnikov. He had a spring cold the day he told Lana, but thinking of the Cassettes going green had him cackling between coughs. Lana was going over today for a congratulatory glass of champagne (no more bourbon for Dwight) and to hear him jam on the book. He wanted her feedback. And she'd tell him about today's interview, *Vanity Fair*. He loved the inside track. He loved glitz. And he'd be happy for her, happy it was "one of us" getting a leg up. As far as he was concerned, why shouldn't they have their turn at power?

Lana was glad to be seeing Dwight, but she was feeling that pleasant pull now, that eagerness to get home to Sam. She decided she wouldn't stop for towels, she'd do that tomorrow. Maybe she'd bring Sam with her, he'd be fine as long as they were in and out, because then he wouldn't feel too domesticated. He was not a man who liked browsing in big stores. But he did like living together, Lana could tell. And when they'd finally talked about why he hadn't said anything those two months, that horrible June and July, he was sheepish. Lana was sitting on his lap looking at him and Sam said, "I was hoping the whole thing would blow over."

"Blow over?! You knew I was waiting."

"Well, it's kind of like going to the doctor, you keep postponing it 'til you run out of excuses."

"And when I confronted you on the sidewalk? What were you thinking then?"

"Uh-oh, the jig is up." They were both laughing. She gripped the hair at the nape of his neck.

"But aren't you happy now?" she asked, jiggling her hand so his head jiggled too.

"Yeah, I guess."

"Well, don't sound too excited."

"I don't want you to think you're running the show, even though you are."

Lana wanted more.

"But didn't you see how sad I was getting?"

"I didn't know that was about us." And then he pulled her close. "As if I'd let you move on . . ." Then he motioned her off his lap 'cause five minutes was the limit his legs could take.

In three months, it would be a year living together. Maybe she'd bring up the M-word then, in September—they could be engaged by Christmas, and the wedding next spring or summer. But a year sounded rote, unromantic. And Sam had softened. The respect she'd shown his slowness, the fact that she'd given him more than his measure of time, it was coming back in spades. He'd loosened up, was following her lead. Maybe she'd just improvise the next step, play it by ear, listen for the right moment. Their apartment (in a building with lots of families) would hold them for three, four years. It had a separate butler's pantry (with a window) that would be big enough for a crib. It could be converted (Lana didn't see why not) if Sam was adamant about keeping his study. He needed his bit of bachelor space, even if it was only an illusion.

Lana took a last sip of coffee. At this minute, she thought, everything is enough. My ducks are all in a row. And because she was the only one at the counter, she began to breathe a song she and Livia had listened to over and over and over in the dark, both of them loving the bang-up finish with its twists on the title, everything coming up "roses and daffodils," everything . . .

What? She couldn't remember. Stumped, Lana went silently through the song from the start—and still couldn't find the line. She put two dollars down next to her coffee cup and waved a little good-bye to the man behind the counter. As she pushed through the glass door, the bell rang. "Sunshine and Santa Claus!"

There it was, all before her.

CHAPTER EIGHTEEN

Look Again

Iris didn't want to get out of the car. She loved the silence gliding through Manhattan at the crack of dawn, gray coming up ghostly under the night's black blue, still too dark to guess what the day would be. She was intrigued with the little brick houses she was sliding by in parts of Queens she'd never seen before. Had she ever actually been to Queens, except for taking planes? The driver was heading toward Far Rockaway, just beyond Kennedy Airport, to a place called Jamaica Bay.

"It's a publicity thing, impromptu," said arts anchor and sorority sister Victoria Pines when she called two weeks earlier. Vicki was roped into it because of her past reporting on animal issues, and now she was roping in Iris. "There's a move to put bike paths in Jamaica Bay, this nature reserve most New Yorkers have never heard of. As if this city needs one more inch of asphalt! A bunch of bird-watchers and friends are trying to nip it in the bud. We're meeting there on October fourteenth, a Saturday—and we need more bodies, some high profiles. I'll have one camera, do some interviews, and then we'll do a quick bird-watch or whatever. Home by noon. You *must come.* It makes sense—because of your nests!"

Iris couldn't say no. Vicki had done such a nice, if predictably hypey, three minutes on Iris's show at **flow** ("These aren't your mother's lamp shades" and "The white gloves have come off" and "If Sylvia Plath used sticks instead of words," et cetera, to which Iris could only think, *oy*).

"Plus," Vicki went on, "there will be at least two eligible bachelors in the group. Jeff Henderson, the newspaperman from Chicago, *still* a blond god and between marriages! And Chip Parks, a Wall Street family. He's a little chubby. But *cute*—a *cute* personality."

Double *oy.* Since Iris's opening in September, since the five inches of puzzled enthusiasm in the *Times,* the tiny ten-sentence rave in *The New Yorker,* the dashing portrait in *Town & Country,* Lana Burton's lyrical spotlight in *VF,* and that vicious sneer in *The Voice* ("Congratulations," Emily Edwards beamed, "someone hates you!"), Vicki was calling constantly. It was as if she decided she had underestimated Iris, as if she saw her in a new light (a fellow "star") and was making her a pet project (the girl she'd guide through Page Six to the prince's castle). Vicki just couldn't comprehend being alone.

But getting into the car that morning, the street asleep in shadow and lamplight—that eerie in-between feeling—it had reminded Iris of hunt days. Up before dawn, the silent bustle in the chill barn, bare lightbulbs blazing in coronas of cold, and the horses clipped and braided, waiting in wool blankets, the big vans parked outside, waiting. And Iris herself. At fifteen, she wasn't yet pretty, but in a black bowler hat and white stock tie her long thin nose over her prim little mouth found a proper context. And her long skinny legs, endlessly embarrassing in skirts, were in black leather boots with black patent tops enviously elegant.

The town car pulled into a parking lot dotted with other town cars, BMWs, and some of those sports vehicles. Iris hoped her outfit was okay. Walking up to the visitors' center, she approached her reflection in the glass doors: Timberland shoes, corduroys rolled to the ankle, a thick taupe turtleneck, and her father's beautiful old shooting jacket. She'd taken it in those first glacial days after his death, slipped it from his closet where the clothes had stopped breathing, so that her mother wouldn't send it off without thinking to an uncle or the Goodwill. It was caramel tweed, and because it was quite large, size forty-two, Iris belted it tight, like a Hemingway wife. She entered the empty center and saw people gathered just beyond a second set of glass doors, in a clearing outside, on the other side of the building. They wore black microfiber, polar fleece, Gore-Tex. Iris sighed. Somehow I'm always a little in left field. Two shiny-haired, East Side twentysomethings stood out especially in their tight-tight pants of god-knew-what fiber, hems falling long over cowboy boots. Where are the cows? wondered Iris, watching the gals cast sassy "how did we get here?" looks around them. More birds, she thought, for Henderson and Parks.

Iris stood looking through the glass. I'm not here to be the life of the party, I'm here as a favor to pain-in-the-neck Vicki. The sun was coming in. The day was going to be gorgeous. Vicki spotted Iris and was on her like a tick.

"Biddle. You're here!"

"Well, of course I'm here," she said, thinking, I came in the car you sent. Vicki was in full light makeup, blond hair pulled back safari style. Her camera guy was nowhere in sight, probably sneaking a cigarette behind a tree. "I've already done two quickies, have two more. But let me introduce you. I don't want you standing alone." Vicki gave Iris the usual once-over. "You're so old-fashioned. But charming," she added quickly.

Dragged by the elbow, pushed up under Jeff Henderson's chiseled nose and piercing blue eyes, made to chat with cute Chip (from the school of sockless-'til-Christmas Wasps), Iris did her best to be sociable, saying yes, how wonderful it was to have an exhibition, and no, despite her nest shades she was not a bird-watcher, though it was lovely to be out this morning. When she finally broke free from Vicki's grip, she drifted over to a notebook on a rough wood podium. It listed recent sightings.

100 American Coot
Northern Harrier
17 Black Crowned Night Heron
Golden Plover!!!!

Nearby, a handsome young man who looked like the guide was setting up a telescope, tightening the legs of a tripod while talking to two older men out of L.L.Bean (more her style). It wasn't that Iris had anything against Jeff Henderson's Holly-wood good looks, his oh-so-piercing eyes (he couldn't help that). There was no question he was a catch for someone, a golden boy grown up, an accomplished man. It's just that the women he married had all been rich. And the women he dated, if they weren't rich, they'd been involved with rich men. Iris found it unsavory, this thing about money. And Chip. Iris didn't care if he was chubby (though Erich had been a rail), but he did seem young ("Thirty-eight," Vicki insisted, "is not too young"). And even if he had been old enough, he was just so exactly what he was—Top-Siders in summer, Belgian Shoes in winter, the parents on Fifth, the sailboat in Maine, cuff links by Schlumberger, lamb shank from Lobel's. He was bred for the luxury life narrowly defined. The woman he needed would be thus bred too—a wife who might want an Iris Original, but never one of the nests.

Iris knew she fell between the cracks. Socially sophisti-cated but solitary. Well-off-seeming but stretching every check (though things were better since the exhibition). And now, was she a lamp shade maker or an artist? Men couldn't get a grip. No woman in her forties was a simple sell, but you could still be smart about marketing. Iris just wasn't. She was too reti-cent, too interior, expected too much. Well, the courtliness she expected hadn't been too much in the early eighties, when she was in her twenties, but men weren't courtly anymore. Worse still, her daughterliness, that trust, pushed up unbidden, like a plant mistaking a slant of light for sun—ever so wrong for men today, and wrong for her age. She tamped it down, on guard against that stirring, but it was there inside her, what she was.

While Iris pondered the list, the three men's voices sifted in: What's in the East Pond? Avocet's gone. I couldn't find it either. But a Hudsonian, two pecs. Are the coots still there? About fifty. And a young peregrine. Heading down to the hawk watch? After this. Northeast winds. Gonna be great. They had two goldens yesterday. Wish I could go.

They had a golden plover right here too, thought Iris, but kept her mouth shut. She fished her binoculars out of her pocket, well actually, they were opera glasses. But good ones. Leicas. She'd bought them last year after her hundredth headache with those antique mother-of-pearls. While the group, waiting for Vicki to finish her spots, milled and chatted, compared what they were doing after the walk, Iris focused her binoculars on branches overhead—sycamore—fiddling with the right eye. She saw motion on a bough and swung over for practice, finding nothing but a blur. She kept trying, finding nothing. These glasses were fine at the opera, but out here they were silly, Lilliputian. What a tenderfoot she was. When it came to the outdoors, there was nothing more ridiculous than bad gear. She felt a tap on her shoulder and turned around.

"I think you should use these," he said, one of the three bird men, handing her a pair of binoculars labeled Zeiss. "Those are nice little Leicas"—he nodded toward her minis— "for Wagner."

"But I can't take your binoculars," Iris said, noticing he had another pair around his neck, noticing his rather blue-green eyes. There was something about him, something familiar.

"They're a spare," he said. "Just keep the strap around your neck." She put it around her neck.

"You'll see things you never saw before." Then with a tug at the tweed sleeve of her jacket he turned away saying, "and no shooting allowed" and walked off. He had that slow flow walk of men who are outdoors a lot alone.

She looked down at the Zeisses, weighty against her chest. She lifted them, and focused. O brave new world, that has such vision in't! She could see the dried veins in a dead leaf, could count the needles on an evergreen tip, and when she swung to a sparrow on the ground, she locked onto it immediately. Its legs were pink.

The bird group was grouping. The leader was giving his spiel. They were originally going to do the circle, which was about a mile around, with the bay along the outside, and a pond on the inside. But since they were starting late, and so many in the group were heading off to the country, they would only walk to the Terrapin Trail and back. He told them about the habitat, why bike paths would be bad (because turtles nested near the road, and cement gets so much hotter than sand). He handed out binoculars to anyone who needed them, and urged everyone to use the spotting scopes. As the group moved off, about twenty in all, the two gals edged toward Henderson. He was murmuring politics with a *Time* writer carrying a scope—their heads bent at the exact same angle. Chip Parks was looking jolly, occasionally whispering to a blowsy brunette with a little Louis Vuitton backpack. Vicki had three men in tow, client friends of her husband, all geared up. She kept leaning and laughing against one of them—the very good-looking one—who let her lean.

The morning was magnificent, a smacking brightness, the

air cold, but not too cold, shot through with sun. At this hour on a hunt morning, about eight-thirty A.M., they'd be at the meet, saddling up in a meadow on grass crunchy with frost, stepping out of their overalls, slipping into black hunt coats, last buff to boots, excited, God how excited they'd be mounting up and becoming high and mighty, one with the history of the hunt, blood up in a blood sport. Iris lifted her chin to the wind. The group, a motley mix of postures, was scanning the rushes in the pond. You couldn't say bird-watching was sartorial.

But the quiet, the quiet at the covert, hounds searching for a scent, was like this. The expectation, eyes and ears sharp, the faraway verging on close-up. Distant ducklike toots on the horn and your horse stamping under you. The black caw of crows above the tree line, the flap of reins as horses shook their heavy necks, bothered by braids sewn in the day before. The etiquette of the field called for quiet. You began to hear everything.

"I-ris," Vicki called, breaking the spell and turning heads. Iris kept her face to the rushes, but heard too well the scuff of gravel as Vicki made her way over. Iris, as nicely as she could, mouthed "What?"

"Why are you over here?" Vicki demanded in a hoarse but at least low whisper. "I want you near me so I can push you into situations." She hooked her fingers around Iris's belt. "I want you to talk to Jeff Henderson."

"I already talked to him," Iris whispered back. "Now I'm looking for birds." It sounded funny. Iris wasn't sure how to look for birds (she was better with branches), except to stare hard at the distance, and to track anything that moved. The leader was saying something about ducks, which surprised Iris. Could ducks be interesting? The woman with the Louis Vuitton backpack looked through a scope, then straightened up saying, "But I don't see duck à l'orange." There was a ripple of laughter and a long-suffering nod from the group leader.

"Who's that?" Iris whispered.

"She's in a production of *The Birds*, off-Broadway, don't ask."

Meanwhile, the two older men, having walked on ahead as if fed up with inane chatter, were leaning into their scopes.

"Got anything?" called the leader.

"Hooded mergansers."

The group began its amble over.

Iris understood that Vicki was trying to be helpful, she really did. But she'd had it with the pushing.

"Vicki, you're a darling matchmaker, but this isn't the time or place." Besides, Iris wanted to see the hooded merganser. She hurried along, walking right up to the scope of the man who had lent her the binoculars.

He immediately stepped back for her.

"The focus is here," he said, pointing to a band around the middle of the scope. She turned it. When the blur tightened to crystal clarity, she caught her breath, then exhaled *ohhhh*.

It had a nutmeg, no, pecan brown body, with a black and white chest—Regency colors!—and a spanking white fan on its head. As Iris watched, the fan opened wider, from twelve to three.

"Is that white the hood?" she asked.

"It is," the man answered. "It's mating plumage. His crest."

Iris couldn't get enough of the pretty thing, the stripes near its tail, its needle beak, its midget crest majestic like a chess knight, then suddenly felt she'd been at the scope too long with this man watching her. She stepped back to let someone else look, but saw that the group was taking turns on the other scopes and it was just the two of them. He moved in, repositioned the scope.

"Here's the female hooded. Not nearly the dandy he is." Iris looked at the reddish brown creature, trying to appreciate the differences, but really wanting to see the male again.

"Can we look at the male once more?"

"You like him." It was a statement that almost seemed a question. He adjusted the scope.

Iris leaned in again, and as she turned the focus she teased, "Are you nearsighted, or far?"

"Hey," he said. But when he returned to the scope, he confessed, "I'm nearsighted. But not *that* bad."

He was scanning very slowly. As he scanned Iris studied his profile, attentive to the sharp, attractive wrinkles at his eye. Where and when? She cast back through New York. Further back to Erich, science, Penn—like digging for something in an old coat pocket, like focusing in the dark, closing in . . .

There. And then. Iris knew as he turned his head and caught her staring.

She blushed. A rush of pink heat, even her ears hot. His smile deepened his wrinkles.

"Iris Biddle," he said. "We've met before. You probably don't remember."

Iris let him continue.

"It was at Penn. In 1989. The dinner for Briansky."

"The big grant he got," Iris said. Eleven years ago.

"Yes. My company awarded that grant. You were there with your husband."

Erich had acted badly that night. No scenes, but the bitterness was beginning, his baiting and obstinance, his turning away. Ned Briansky was hail-fellow, smooth, a very smart operator, and an MD/PhD, which meant he could do clinical work—bigger bang for the buck. Erich didn't need the grant for himself, but it enraged him that doctors were handed money for repetitive projects ("busy work" he jeered), while PhDs had to scrounge to make breakthroughs. At any rate, Iris wouldn't hear Erich criticized.

"That would make you Bill Warren," she said. Warbucks, to Erich. He founded Z-Tech Pharmaceuticals. A small company, suddenly big with three key patents in the early eighties. He had less hair now, shorter, silver, he'd filled out some. The old khakis completed the camouflage. But that night he had been The Benefactor, polished in a dark blue suit and a self-important dress shirt, a concentrated five foot eight with a hard drive behind a quick smile and eyes that missed nothing. She remembered the introduction, the cold zone between him and Erich when the two shook hands, the thrusting manner of their short conversation, and then those eyes on her so that she drew herself up. She'd noted the contrast with Erich, so rumpled and skinny and tall, his jacket open and swinging, and had preferred Erich's grace. Because he was hers. But Warren's taut vigor, his bristling energy, was undeniable—his success, he was not yet forty-five, regarded with awe—and having heard Erich complain about him, and then finally meeting him, it was one of those moments all wives know when they see what their husband hates and feel themselves dissenting, feel themselves thinking, *You could use more of that.*

"Erich was brilliant," he said. "With a very protective wife. I still remember the frosty look you gave me that night. In that blue dress."

Iris was stunned. That blue dress, almost lavender, a sleeveless column of silk velvet—this man remembered it.

"I wasn't very fair that night," she said.

"The spouse doesn't have to be fair."

"The funny thing was people thought Erich so dismissive. But actually, he took everything so hard."

"Research was tough in the eighties—a heartbreaker. You had to get the data and go, fast and arrogant. I know I was. Your husband was too. Today it's even worse. And one way or another, you pay for arrogance."

"He's in the Peace Corps now. Testing drugs in the field. He's happy. Happy as he's wired to be."

She realized they were behind the group, and was self-conscious. She did not see a ring on his finger, but then, the talk in those days was that his marriage wasn't working.

"That wasn't the last time our paths crossed either," he continued.

"No?"

"Iris Originals. I understand you're doing something else now. But there was a point where my wife—my second wife—had to have one and couldn't get one. She was wait listed." He was amused. "Waiting is not something Jennifer knew how to do. She wanted that damn lamp shade. Like a stuck record. And all the time I'm thinking—The Blue Dress strikes again."

Iris was elated, more than she should be, and trying not to show it.

"People really don't like to wait," she agreed, not wanting to seem gloating, and then both of them were crowded by a vague honking in the distance that was no longer vague but coming straight at them from above—a V of geese winging in low for a landing, so low they felt the raucous *whoosh*. He was shaking his head at the folly—though whether it was Jennifer or the lamp shade or the geese or all three, Iris couldn't tell. She was laughing.

"And where is Jennifer now?" Iris asked. She couldn't help asking and why shouldn't she ask.

"I hear"—he bumped the scope to his shoulder—"she's about to marry someone else. Whoever he is I wish him the best." He raised his eyebrows. "He'll need it."

"Bill."

"I know. I shouldn't have said that. Come on."

They walked about twenty yards until something stopped him. He planted the scope and focused. She stood quietly, contemplating the fleet of geese just settled at the pond's edge, then felt his fingers curl around her arm, firm through jacket and sweater, floating her toward him, to the scope, then his hand resting on her back, for a second. Leaning in, hardly breathing, her right eye up at the lens, Iris saw a fat gray bird, with a black forehead, a long beak, and a hunchy posture. It had a big red eye.

"What is it?" she asked, excited by his nearness.

"A black-crowned night heron, mature."

"*I love him,*" cried Iris, still in the scope, "he's like a fat banker in a pearl gray morning suit. *Come look again.*"

She wanted Bill to look again so he could see how right she was, but instead he was looking at her with that stricken softness men get out of nowhere. When you say something that thrums a chord, or maybe it was the way you said it, or something they never thought they'd hear. You never knew because they never tell. Her heart knocked hard and she stepped back. He came to the scope and looked again.

"Are you here because you know Vicki?" she asked.

"No. I don't know Noisy. Though seeing she's your friend . . ."

"She's a sorority sister," Iris stated as he straightened up, "which is not the same thing at all. But you were saying."

"One of the guys called last night. He knew I was going down to Cape May today and asked if I'd stop here on the way. I sold my shares in the company four years ago. Now I spend my time in wetlands preservation, getting more land into conservancies. I'm here a lot."

"But that must be wonderful work."

"It is. Frustrating too." His eyes caught above her. "*Quick.*" he turned her around to see a brown bullet shoot by. "Merlin," he said.

It was fast. It was thrilling.

"It's a falcon. Amazing flyer. Like a peregrine, but smaller."

"Merlin," Iris said. She tried to catch him in her binoculars, had him in view for about one second, then nothing. When the merlin came up again they watched it with their eyes, watched it dive and climb and bank and dive again. Then it was gone.

The group was gone too.

"They're on the Terrapin Trail," Bill said. "Do you want to join them?"

"No."

"Let's head back then."

The path was mute under the bleaching sun as they walked side by side in the day's crisp winds. Iris wasn't sure where to look. Were they still bird-watching? She glanced at him and saw he was looking down. He was . . . older. You are the man I should be with, she thought, the man you are now. You're the one I should be with.

"How long does it take to be good at bird-watching?" she asked.

He took a while to answer.

"At first it takes months, just to learn how to look. Then it takes years to know what you're looking for, and damned if you don't seem to be learning it over and over again. But each time you do, you know more. Then one day"—he stopped, he was facing her—"Iris, it's a lifetime."

She touched the binoculars on her chest. "Thank you. For lending me these."

He slid the scope off his shoulder. What was he doing, he was so close, would he touch her again?

He reached for her hand. He held it. "I'll be back on Thursday, and . . . if you're not already busy. How would it be if I took you to dinner Friday night? A Friday night date."

Can life do this—happiness pressing upon her? Just hand you a morning, a path, a man? Of course you didn't know what would happen, what would or wouldn't come next. But Iris did know. She knew. Because of what was already there in his blue-green eyes trying not to look at her too much, but looking now, and his hand not letting hers go. How would it be? Iris simply had to, simply couldn't, stop smiling.

"It would be"—Lord, she was going to owe Vicki—"heaven."